Blaze

By

Ronna M. Bacon

Deuteronomy 31:6 Be strong and of a good courage, fear not, nor be afraid of them: for the LORD your God, he it is that does go with you; he will not fail you, nor forsake you.

Psalm 18:1-2 I will love You, O Lord, my strength. The Lord is my rock and my fortress and my deliverer; My God, my strength, in whom I will trust; My shield and the horn of my salvation, my stronghold.

Table of Contents

Chapter 1

The late afternoon summer air hung heavy and oppressive. The sky had a brassy look to it that meant thunderstorms at some point even though there were no clouds in the sky. David Framer stopped to wipe a suit-coated arm across his forehead, the change from air conditioning to the outdoor heat and humidity almost more than he could handle. It had been a long day dealing with lawyers and clients who just didn't want to agree to what they had signed up for. That always meant more stress on David or Blaze as he was commonly called by his friends.

Blaze walked slowly towards his nondescript white SUV, not at all a vehicle that a multi-millionaire would drive. But that was Blaze. His money was used for other things. He kept enough to be comfortable but didn't want the showy lifestyle that others had and which only mean danger and more stress.

His key fob in his hand, Blaze hit the bottom to open the hatch of the vehicle and then raised it. His brown leather briefcase hit the floor inside before he was reaching for the blue and white striped tie. Pulling it from around his neck, he tucked it into a pocket of his navy blue suit jacket before said jacket was pulled off and dropped on top of the briefcase. Blaze rolled up the sleeves of his once-crisp white shirt even as he looked around. Today had not gone as he had planned. It was to have been an easy, relaxing day until the trouble with the client meant an all-day meeting.

Shutting the hutch, Blaze's hand hesitated for a moment. He could feel the heat shimmering up from the pavement under his feet. All he wanted to do was to find his back deck, a cold bottle of water on the table beside him, and enjoy the coolness that came from the trees surrounding his cabin. He lived in the forest by choice, a choice that he had never regretted.

A soft sound or even what he might consider a sob caught at Blaze's attention. This was a private parking lot, he knew, connected to his building and his company. There should be no one around. He spun in a circle, a hand up to shade his eyes, as he sought to find out where the sound was coming from. Rapid footsteps took Blaze towards a vehicle parked near the outside gate, a vehicle that should not be there. His head tilted as he drew closer, the sound of his footsteps not drawing the attention of the two men who were shouting and gesturing wildly. Blaze drew in a deep breath as he saw the woman huddled against the car, her arms covering her head. He could hear the faint sobs as she tried to shrink even more into the car body and was not able to do that.

Blaze sighed. This is not how he wanted to end an extremely stressful day but it was not in him to walk away from anyone in trouble, let alone a female. Without hesitation, he reached around the men for the woman's arm, drawing her towards him. He wrapped an arm around her, realizing that this was a lady, just not a female. And she was scared, no terrified, he thought.

"There you are, darling. I wondered where you were." His arm tightened around her, even as the wind

—

picked up and blew his black hair into his deep gray eyes. Those eyes took in briefly the deep red hair and violet eyes of the lady tucked tight to him. He could see the sprinkle of freckles across her face as she looked up briefly before her attention went back to the men in front of them.

The men stared at Blaze in shock before one of them reached for the lady. Blaze's arm blocked the man's hand even as he tucked her behind him.

"You're on private property." Blaze's face was stern. "You need to leave." He watched at the men exchanged a look and then saw the anger and violence growing in them. He was afraid that he would be unable to protect the lady before she disappeared.

"Not happening, pal. She's coming with us." The second man stepped to walk around Blaze, finding Blaze stepping backwards, forcing the lady to do the same.

Blaze felt digging into his back as she clutched at his shirt. He gave a grim smile as the men continued to advance on him and try to reach for the lady behind him. Blaze would not let that happen. He heard other footsteps approaching and prayed that God had sent help. He couldn't contend with more than the two in front of him.

"Mr. Framer?" The security guards had approached quietly, not sure what was happening other than there were trespassers on their property. The security guard on the desk inside the building had already reached out to the police.

"Joseph? These gentlemen need to be detained. They are trespassing. They are also harassing a guest of ours." Blaze's voice was firm and crisp. The guards were familiar with his tones of voice and knew that he was angry.

"We can do that." Joseph and two of the guards simply reached to handcuff the men despite their protests.

Blaze watched carefully, knowing that this was a dangerous point in the confrontation. He turned slightly, his arm wrapping around the lady before he was walking rapidly away to tuck her inside his vehicle. He reached for the bottle of water one of the guards was handing him, uncapping it and handing it to her. She seemed reluctant to take it before Blaze's hand reached to wrap hers around the bottle.

Standing back from the vehicle, Blaze watched the commotion as the men resisted being arrested. He shook his head, turning to walk around his vehicle. Sliding behind the wheel, he started the vehicle, his fingers tapping at the steering wheel. Blaze shifted on his seat to study the lady, finding that she just would not look at him.

"My name is David Framer. Friends call me Blaze. May I have your name?" Blaze felt as if he was being overly formal but given the circumstances, he felt he had to. He waited patiently for her to respond.

A soft voice finally answered, barely loud enough to be heard.

"I'm Bevin Connors. I need to leave. They'll hurt you." She reached for the door handle, jumping as Blaze rested his hand on her arm.

"No, you can come with me." Before Bevin could say anything, Blaze drove, suddenly desperate to get this beautiful lady somewhere safe. He was well aware that someone from the police department would be in touch. Blaze didn't see the car that pulled away from the curb as he drove off and followed him. He was too concerned about the lady who was shifting on the seat beside him.

Chapter 2

Turning off his vehicle as he watched the garage door close behind him, Blaze was torn. He had this beautiful lady in the vehicle with him who seemed to want to be anywhere but there. But he could feel the danger that surrounded her and didn't want any harm to come to her. He shifted on his seat before he was out of the vehicle and around it to open her door, a hand reaching out to help her out. Bevin stared at his hand and then at him before she tentatively reached out to take his, an uncomfortable smile on her face. Blaze sighed. This was not how his day was to end but it seemed as if God had other plans for his day.

"In this way, Bevin, if I may call you that. Mary, my housekeeper, will look after you." He grinned at her, his teeth showing white against his tan. "Don't be afraid of us. We mean you no harm." Blaze could see the way that she relaxed as he said those words.

Bevin stared up at him, wondering at his height. She didn't know if she had ever met someone as tall as him. For now, she felt safe but she knew that wouldn't last. It never did. If anyone stepped in to help her, they were either scared off or hurt. Bevin was tired of being on the run and looking over her shoulder, fear driving her from town to town. She had left behind just about everything that she owned in the last town before she headed for this town. And even how, the ratty and worn backpack that she had carried was lost somewhere.

"I don't have my backpack. I need it." Bevin's voice was barely audible as she struggled with tears. Angry at herself for crying, Bevin swiped at her cheeks, not seeing the compassion that showed on Blaze's face or on that of Marry as she stood in the kitchen, watching Blaze enter.

"It's okay, Bevin. Mary will find you something. She collects new clothing for a shelter near here. She'll just raid that pile."

"Oh, she can't do that. They will be expecting them." Bevin jumped as she felt arms around her in a hug and then a prayer whispered in her ear, a prayer just for her.

"Not at all, love. They didn't know that the clothes are here. In fact, they would tell you to take them. Now, I don't know about you, but on a hot, sticky day like this, I like to have a shower or a bath just to freshen up. We'll let you do that and then find something for you to eat." Mary led Bevin away, albeit somewhat reluctantly on Bevin's part.

Blaze watched her walk away, a troubled look on his face. Out to the garage and back quickly, he dropped his briefcase in his office and then headed for a shower and a change of clothes. Pulling a blue t-shirt over his head and down over the jean shorts that he had on, Blaze paused. He sighed. He knew that Frank would be around as an investigating officer. Anything that happened at his office warranted that even though he had protested numerous times.

Walking back through his comfortable and sprawling home, he could hear low conversation coming from the bedroom where Anna was talking with Bevin. Art, Mary's husband, looked around as Bevin hit the kitchen doorway in a rapid manner, a frown on his face.

"Blaze? What have you gone and done this time?" Spoken somewhat in jest, Art waited for Blaze to respond. He frowned at the younger man before he began to pray for him. Somehow, Art decided that Blaze had just taken off on one of those adventures that his friends seemed to have needed to have.

"I don't know, Art. She was being confronted by two men in the parking lot. I just couldn't let that happen." Blaze had a little boy tone to his voice, one Art recognized from when Blaze was small and wanted either his parents or Mary and himself to understand why he had stood up for someone.

"I know you couldn't, Blaze. Who's coming to talk with you?" Art handed Blaze a glass of lemonade and then pointed to one of the stools at the counter. "Sit, Blaze. Let me pray with you. I think you have just walked into something."

Blaze sighed, knowing that was truly the case. He turned as he heard soft footsteps and was on his own feet, heading for the hallway. He paused for a moment before he simply wrapped Bevin into a hug, feeling her arms hugging him back.

Leaning back, Blaze studied the lady in his arms. He was deeply worried about her without knowing why. That was a conversation that he would need to have with her. He sighed. Obviously that would not happen tonight. Blaze had sent a quick text message off to his secretary, simply stating that he would be working from home the next day. It was something that he did frequently, needing to be away from the office at times just to let his staff work as they needed to. They appreciated his consideration for them.

"Mary and Art have a light meal for us, Bevin. Come. You can eat, if you wish to. Then we would like to spend time in prayer with you. God placed you here in my home for now." Blaze watched as she looked up at him, wonder crossing her face briefly before she shuttered her emotions.

"Thank you. I'm not really that hungry." Bevin moved away from Blaze, stopping as she saw Art. She frowned at him. "I saw you today."

"You did?" Art grinned at her. "And where would that have been?"

"You were leaving that building." Bevin spun to stare at Blaze. "You were the last one to leave."

"I was. It's my building that you were at, Bevin. We'll talk tomorrow. For tonight, it is enough that you are fed and then find your sleep. It's okay. You should be safe here. I have good security." Blaze didn't continue, not wanting to admit that he was a multi-millionaire and needed good security.

Bevin finally sat at the counter, not sure that she should. A quiet thank you came from her as a plate of food was set in front of her. She jumped as Blaze reached for her hand, his head bowing as he said a simply blessing on their food.

Blaze watched Bevin carefully, seeing how fragile she now seemed. There was a sense of danger that surrounded her. He shared a look with Art, seeing his subtle nod. Blaze sighed again. He had no idea what he had just gotten mixed up in but God had placed him there to protect Bevin. He just had no idea how entwined their lives would become.

Chapter 3

A sudden loud bang at the front door had Blaze on his feet and heading that way. The smoke that greeted him choked off his breath and sent him to the floor, to lie unconscious. Bevin screamed as the men rushed inside before she too slumped to the floor. Neither one saw the bodies of Mary and Art as they sprawled on the kitchen floor, not moving as the men searched around them nor did they see the bodies of Blaze and Bevin hastily gathered from the floor and rushed from the home. They disappeared into a vehicle and said vehicle disappeared down the driveway.

Thirty minutes later, a police vehicle stopped in front of the cabin. Frank, the investigator assigned to the incident but also a good friend of Blaze and his parents, frowned for a moment. Something was off, he could tell.

Walking towards the house, Frank's steps paused as he eyed the shattered front door. A hand reached for his police-issue weapon as he walked that way, eyes and senses alert for anything out of the ordinary. He coughed as he caught the faint remains of the gas or whatever it was that the intruders had used.

Frank drew in a deep breath as he found Mary and Art still sprawled on the kitchen floor. He bent over them and quickly found that they were indeed still alive. He was back to his vehicle calling in more officers and the crime scene techs.

Standing outside of the cabin, Frank studied the area, his eyes on the footprints that entered and then left the house.

"The ones leaving are heavier, Frank." George, another detective, stood beside him, disturbed at what Frank had described.

"They are. That means Blaze has been taken from here." Frank spun to stare back at the cabin. "I know that he brought the lady with him from that incident at the building. She must have been taken as well."

"I would suspect so. How are Mary and Art?" George watched as the paramedics headed away with the couple.

"I don't know. They were still unconscious. When I got here, there was still the smell of smoke or gas of some kind." Frank walked back towards the cabin, staying carefully away from the tracks as much as he could. "I would think that Blaze has been abducted. I just don't know why. And I know nothing about the lady who was with him. The patrol officers who responded to the incident at his building didn't have that information. Blaze moved her out of there and to what he thought was safety."

Frank walked through the halls of the town's hospital, feeling as if he had done that too many times lately for friends. He was exhausted, with too many cases to investigate. Ones that involved friends always took more out of all of them. Blaze had been a good friend over the years as had his parents. All of them supported the police force and other emergency

———

services quietly and in the background. None of them flaunted the wealth that had been first inherited and then grown.

"Doc? What can you tell me?" Frank paused at the room where he saw Art.

"Some time of gas, I suspect, Frank." The physician turned. "There's not a lot of evidence now as to what it was. Whatever it was? Art said that it overtook them quickly. He's worried about Blaze, though, and a lady?"

Frank nodded. He was worried as well. He just didn't have enough information to know where to turn or what to think.

"There is a lady involved. Blaze came to her assistance today and took her to Mary." Frank headed for Art and saw that the man was now sleeping. He sighed. When he approached Mary's stretcher, it was the same. He walked away from the hospital, not sure where to turn or who to talk to.

George had been around, he knew, and was waiting for him. Handing Frank a cup of coffee, which he knew was badly needed, George simply waited.

"What do you think, George?" Frank was puzzled as to what had happened.

"I have no idea, Frank. They have just vanished. And that's not Blaze. He just wouldn't have walked away from Mary and Art. And he certainly would not have put the lady in any more danger."

"No, he wouldn't have. And Jerry says there isn't much evidence to gather. The men, whoever they are, were very careful." Frank sighed. "This is getting old."

"It is. What Ashlynn and her nieces went through was enough. We don't need this with Blaze." George sighed this time as he pulled out his phone and squinted at it in the dimming light. "Jerry found something that he's not sure of. He'll work it through and then contact us."

"And he will. He's like a terrier with that, never letting go until he sorts everything out." Frank dropped his empty cup into a nearby trash container. "Head on home, George. We're off the clock until tomorrow. Maybe by that time, Blaze and the lady will be home."

George snorted, knowing full well that was likely wishful thinking.

"You too, Frank. Sue's waiting dinner for you more than likely."

"She would be." Frank could only stand for a few moments, petitioning God for his friend and the lady whose name he didn't know. He prayed that by tomorrow, Mary and Art would be able to at least give them that name.

Mary was on her feet not long after Frank had walked away. She shook off the hands that tried to keep her in her room, searching for Art. He was on his feet as well, looking for her. The couple walked out of the hospital and found an officer willing to drive them home and then remain outside of Blaze's cabin for the night.

―

20

"What happened, Art?" Mary worked at cleaning up the kitchens, uncertain as to what happened.

"It was gas of some kind, love. Blaze I think had heard something at the door and was on his feet heading that way. I don't remember much after that." Art paused, a frown on his face. "It seems as if whoever was at the door just walked away with Blaze and Bevin."

"They did. We need to find them." Mary reached for her phone, scrolling through her messages. "Nothing here." She frowned once more. "Blaze's phone?"

"On his desk. He left it there to charge just as he does every night. We have no way to contact him."

Chapter 4

Frank walked away from his conversations with both Mary and Art, frustrated that he was no further ahead in his quest for answers. Neither could remember much of what had happened the night before. Frank had also taken to the streets of Grasspoint, looking for answers. The street people were silent, telling him that they either didn't know anything or that they were afraid of whoever it was. If they knew, he was well aware that they would approach him. Blaze and his charities helped out too many of them for any of them to walk away without helping him.

Searching the town, no one was able to find Blaze or Bevin. By now, Frank had her name and was investigating her. He was not liking what he was hearing from another jurisdiction. Bevin had approached the officers there, asking for help. She was being stalked, she stated, and they had found evidence of that. Unfortunately, she had abruptly left town without leaving any address or information where they could reach her at. Their question to Frank was whether he could find her or not. They were dismayed and almost angered when they found out how she had disappeared.

Two days had passed since the abduction. Blaze's father, Brody, had been around, conferring with Frank. He had no idea who might have wanted to abduct his son. It was something that they constantly worried about and monitored and had all of Blaze's life. His mother, Emily, had also cornered Frank one day, plainly stating that Blaze was in danger and asking what he was doing about it. Frank had grinned at her, hugged her as she was a great friend of his, and walked away. He had no idea how to answer her. No one did.

Three days later, Blaze stumbled as he walked towards his cabin through his woods. His arm was tight around Bevin as he held her upright. They had both been ill-used, beatings on the second day of captivity. Somehow though, they had managed to walk away from their abductors. Blaze was never sure afterwards how they managed that but God had intervened. His constant prayer had been for God's protection and for a way to escape and bring the beautiful lady whom he decided that he loved to safety.

His hand fumbled at the door latch before he was able to work it and shove the door open. He stumbled instead, barely keeping to his feet, his arm tightening around Bevin to guide her with him. Blaze lost his fight to keep upright as the door swung shut behind him. His eyes rolled upwards as he collapsed to the dark hardwood floor, taking Bevin with him. Neither of the couple moved as Mary and Art hurried towards the front of the house, hearing the door open and not expecting anyone and then hearing the sound of bodies hitting the floor. They feared the worst.

Art was on his knees beside the couple, reaching to assess them, even as Mary ran for her phone to call for help. Back beside Art and on her knees as well, she stared at Blaze.

"Where did he come from?" Her voice sounded loud in the silence and she winced at that.

"I don't know, love, but they're home. And help will be here soon." Art was on his feet as he heard the sirens cut off and opened the door.

Frank almost ran towards the cabin. He had not expected either of the couple to show up at all. It wasn't what happened. Standing beside Art who had an arm around Mary, Frank opened and then closed his mouth.

"Art? Where did they come from?"

"I have no idea. We were in the kitchen and heard the front door. It shouldn't have opened. By the time we got there, they were on the floor and not responding."

Frank watched closely as the couple were assessed before being lifted to stretchers and then wheeled away. He sent officers with them, not sure what to think. He would follow them to the hospital shortly. For now, he was at Blaze's home, trying to determine just where the couple had been and why they had appeared as they did.

Walking through the hospital waiting room towards the emergency ward, Frank paused. Blaze's parents were there. He hesitated before nodding at them and walking on by. He was intent on finding out how the couple were and what their injuries were. He stayed near the door as he watched the physician examining Blaze.

Turning at last, the physician approached Frank, a hand out to shake Frank's.

"What do we have, Doc?" Frank kept his eyes on his friend, not sure what was going on.

"What do we have? They are both dehydrated and somewhat the worse for that. I don't see that they were abused in any way. Blaze does have a bruise on his jaw, likely from trying to protect the lady. As for Bevin, she is also dehydrated but no obvious signs that she was maltreated." The physician walked away at that, the ward too busy for him spend time in speculation. That wasn't his task, he knew, but he knew Blaze and worried about him. Blaze seemed to have become mixed up in something and whatever that was seemed to involve the lady with him.

Frank nodded before he approached the stretcher. Blaze had roused, staring around the room before his eyes closed. He was safe, or relatively so, he thought. He jumped slightly as he felt a hand touch his shoulder and then heard Frank praying for him.

"Blaze? What can you tell me?" Frank had his notebook and pen out, setting the notebook on the bedside table as he waited patiently for Blaze to respond.

Blaze blinked, trying to concentrate. It was hard, he decided, not having slept for three days and not having anything to eat or drink. He eyed the medical equipment around him and then felt at the intravenous line. It was necessary, Blaze knew, but he hated it. He hated being in the hospital and always had.

"What can I tell you? I don't rightly know, Frank. They took us out when we were unconscious. I don't know that we were that far from my cabin.

They didn't bring in any water or food. In fact, it seems that they just dumped us and left us there. We finally roused enough to be on our feet late last night. Early this morning, God told me the door was open and to leave. We were at the Miller's place. They're away for six months on that mission trip. I would suspect that someone used their home without their permission." Blaze's head went back on the pillow as he slept.

Frank nodded. A K-9 unit had tracked their path back to that house. He was in the process of obtaining a search warrant to go in. For now, he had to speak with Bevin, a lady who he had needed to speak with days earlier but had been prevented from doing that by the disappearance.

He paused in the hallway, hearing the sounds around him from the busy Emergency ward and moving to stay out of the hurried steps of the healthcare personnel. Frank had no idea yet as to why Bevin seemed to be hunted but hunted she certainly was. He had read through the reports from the incident at Blaze's building and the statements from both Art and Mary. That didn't really help much in his investigation. His eyes closed briefly as he leaned against a wall. All he could was pray for his friend and the lady now in his life.

Chapter 5

Standing being another stretcher holding another victim of crime, Frank shook his head. It was almost getting to be too much, he decided. Another friend and a lady involved in something that they had no inkling what it was about. He watched, eyes narrowing, as Bevin stared away from him. She was well aware that he was there. She was ignoring him, hoping he would leave.

Frank gave a small smile. He knew what she was up to. Other victims and witnesses did the same. It wouldn't work, he knew.

"Miss Connors? We do need to speak, not just about why you're here. We have the other day and the incident at Blaze's building to discuss." Frank was not backing down or away from her. He had been an officer too long to do that.

Bevin sighed to herself. He just was not going to leave, she knew. She had to face the officer and give a statement. She turned to face him, expecting to see dislike and censure on his face. Instead, she found compassion and kindness. That had not been her experience in her hometown with the officers.

"I know. I just don't want to." Bevin's fingers rubbed at the blanket. "What do you want to know?"

"First, where are you from and what brought you here?"

"Where am I from? Cairn, a little village an hour from here. And what brought me here? I was running for my life, if you must know. I have no idea who is chasing me or why. I think those two men the other day are part of a group that is after me. Can you help me?" Bevin blinked back tears. She did not cry but seemed to be doing that lately. The terror that she felt was driving that. She kept praying for release from whatever it was but God seemed to be silent on that. Bevin knew better, that God was protecting her but allowing this.

"We can try. We don't like it when ladies are threatened in our town. We do our best to protect them but we do need you to work with us."

"That's not a problem. Talk to Officer Grassie in Hope. He's the one who's been working to determine who is after me. I don't know who it is. As far as I know, I don't have anything someone would want, I haven't seen anything that I shouldn't have, and I haven't heard anything at all."

"That's okay. We'll work through it. Now, did you know the men?"

Bevin shook her head. She had puzzled that through before the abduction and didn't know the men.

"No, I don't. I was running away from them. That's how I ended up in that parking lot. They tried to make me go with them before Mr. Framer intervened. He graciously offered me protection. Only that didn't work out so well. We were taken from his home and then just left in another home. This morning, we were able to walk out of there and he led me to his home again, I think. I don't really remember what

—

happened and it's not clear where we ended up. Do you know?" Bevin studied Frank, seeing his nod.

"I do. You ended up at Blaze's cabin or home. Mary and Art were there and got you help. That's enough for now. You do need to rest. We'll talk again, Bevin. If you need to speak with someone about what you went through, we do have friends who would gladly speak with you." Frank pocketed his pen and walked away, finding Emily standing outside the door waiting for him to finish.

"Frank?" Emily kept her voice low, not wanting to startle the younger lady who was watching her.

"She's hurting, Emily. And she is being chased and hunted. Go on in. She needs a mother right now, I suspect." Frank walked away, leaving Emily staring after him before she walked into the room to stand beside Bevin.

"I'm sorry. I think that you have the wrong room." Bevin was praying that she was wrong, that this lady who seemed to be a mother had indeed come to find her.

"No, I don't think so. May I call you Bevin?" At Bevin's nod, Emily simply hugged the younger lady, finding Bevin clinging to her. A prayer was whispered in Bevin's ear, calming her. "I'm David's mother. You know him as Blaze. He sent me to find you. His father is with him. Now, what can I do for you?" Emily leaned back to look at Bevin, seeing the tears as they started and simply hugged her once more.

―

"I'm sorry. I don't cry." Bevin swiped at her cheeks, taking with a soft thank you the warm wet cloth handed to her and wiping her tears away.

"It's understandable. You have been harassed and threatened, taken to a cabin where you didn't know anyone, and then abducted. Blaze has said a little of what happened to you over the past few days. It's hard to be away from your home and family when you need them, let alone have this happen to you." Emily stepped away from Bevin for a moment before she was back, a glass of water in her hand for the younger lady.

"Thank you. I need my Mom but she's not here. She's on the other side of the country with my Dad. They've been there for a couple of weeks for his work. I can call them but it's not the same." Bevin refused to look up at Emily.

"No, it's not the same. Once we get you out of here and back to Blaze's, then we'll work on contacting them."

"Oh, I can't go back there. I'm too dangerous." Bevin looked up in shock as Emily simply laughed.

"It could be the other way around. Blaze is the president of a multi-million dollar company. He does mostly charity work. So it could be him that's bringing danger to you."

Bevin was vigorously shaking her head. That wasn't right. The men had been after her. She shuddered as she remembered the coarse voices telling her that she had to go with them, that their boss wanted to see her. Bevin just didn't know why.

———

"I don't know why those men wanted me to go with them. I don't know their employer. Can you help me figure this out?" Bevin jumped once more as she felt arms around her and hugging her tightly to a body. She looked up at Blaze. "You shouldn't be on your feet."

"I'm okay, Bevin. Just a little shaky. We'll figure it out. For now, Mom and Dad are heading back for my place. You're welcome to tag along if you like." He grinned down at the lady, realizing that he didn't want her to be anywhere else but beside him. "You may be dangerous. I might be dangerous. How be we be dangerous together?" He laughed at his mother as she swatted his arm and told him to behave. "Besides, God wants us to stay together. And He is protecting us, even though we are going through some hard stuff."

Chapter 6

Moving through his home late that afternoon, Blaze felt uncomfortable. The effects of being abducted from there were still strong. The peace of his home had been shattered and it would take work and his faith in God to restore that. He looked for Bevin, not finding her anywhere. Searching in a more frantic manner, Blaze finally tracked her down on his back porch. She was seated in the swing, the swing in gentle motion, her head back and her eyes closed. Blaze hesitated to approach her but finally did, startling her as he sat.

"You okay?" Blaze's voice was barely audible but his concern for the lady seated beside him was evident.

Bevin shrugged. She had no idea how to feel. She knew that God had protected them. That much was evident as they were still alive. Bevin just wished it had not happened or if it had to have, then it was over and the ones responsible were in custody. That had not happened as far as she knew.

"I have no idea how to feel, Blaze. How am I supposed to? I came to this town, praying that I would be able to stay. It doesn't look as if I am going to be able to." Bevin blinked back tears. She had found the town and its people to be friendly. His parents had stepped in to help, taking the place of her parents for the moment when they could not be there. She had spoken with her mother, tears thickening both of their voices. Her parents were planning on flying back in the next couple of days. Her father's work had wrapped up and they had taken a couple of days just to vacation.

"I don't know how you should feel. I know how I would feel. Scared. Terrified. Alone. Lonely. Confused. Hurting in every way I could.' Blaze grinned at her as she stared at him, finally shutting her mouth.

"About like that." She shifted on the swing so that she faced him more. "What actually do you do, Blaze? Your mom said something about millions of dollars and charities."

Blaze nodded, Bevin was asking the questions that he would if the roles had been reversed. He just didn't know how to explain his occupation or passion.

"Dad inherited a lot of money from my grandparents. They invested early in their marriage and the investments grew. He has continued with those investments. Dad didn't want just to waste the money. He decided to do something that would bring hope and safety and help to others. He was working on his own until I graduated from college. At that point, he decided to set up a company to manage what all we were doing. Our work is charity, Bevin. We don't ask for the money to be repaid but rather that the recipient pay it forward. We have a strict investigative and interrogative approach for anyone who is seeking help. We want to encourage them and not bring them down." Blaze paused for a moment, not sure how to continue. "There is a part of our work that is kept really secret. We help in the beach for missing and exploited children and youth."

Bevin had been listening very carefully to Blaze's words. She nodded to herself. There was that passion in him to help, He had done that with her.

"And you don't want anyone to know that." Bevin reached for Blaze's hand, sensing the fear that was rising within him. "Blaze? What is going on? You're afraid."

Blaze nodded. She had pegged his feelings only too well. He was deeply afraid for this lady and didn't know why. No one had been able to tell him that.

"I am. And I am afraid for you. I have a question for you, Bevin. Where is your home?" Blaze listened to the sounds of nature that echoed in the quiet after his question. His mouth opened to repeat it before he snapped it closed. His eyes were studying the lady with him, wanting to protect her and prevent any more harm from coming to her. It just didn't seem as if it would be possible.

"My home? It was in Greenton but I left there a few years ago. I have been on the move ever since, working in temporary positions. I just haven't been able to find the one town where I feel that I can put down roots. I don't have a lot, just what was in my car. And I have no idea where that is right now. I ran from it when those men began to chase me. I just don't know how I ended up at your building." Bevin's brow wrinkled as she thought through that day. "I was just so scared."

"I know that you were. You almost shut down on us. And then being kidnapped didn't help, did it?" Blaze grinned at her for a moment. "We'll find it.

<hr>

Frank is likely looking for it. Send him the make, model, and license plate number."

Bevin nodded, her thoughts already moving to something different.

"I don't get it, Blaze. Why kidnap us and then let us just walk away. They abused us with how they didn't provide anything for us."

"I know. That's a question I intend to ask them when they are arrested. And they will be arrested. Make no doubt about that. Frank will find them. We just may not like what we have to do through." Blaze drew in a deep breath. "I don't know where you stand with God, Bevin, but He is here with us. He has never left us nor will He ever do that. He was there with us in that building and when we escaped. He wants only the best for us but sometimes His best means leading us through stormy weather and deep waters."

Bevin had turned to him as he spoke, her head nodding as he did so.

"I believe that, Blaze. It doesn't mean that I have to like what I go through. I just have to keep my hand in His and trust. And that is so difficult to do." Bevin shook for a moment in her fear. "When do you go back to work?"

"I work from home some days and have been in touch with my staff. They are well able to carry on daily tasks without me hovering over them. Anything that I need to address? It is couriered here by one of the security guards. It's how we've always worked." Blaze closed his eyes for a moment, exhausted beyond what he had ever been before, he thought. His eyes

---

opened to find Bevin with her own eyes closed. He wasn't sure at this point if she was sleeping or praying. On his feet, he gathered her into his arms, finding her turning into his shoulder and giving a soft sigh. Blaze headed for her bedroom, to gently set her on the bed. Anna was there to cover her. Her eyes flickered between Blaze and Bevin before she nodded. She saw the softened look on Blaze's face, taking away the sternness that usually covered it and bringing it back to more of what she remembered from his youth.

"Go and find your rest, Blaze." Anna hugged him and then sent him on his way. "She'll sleep. And you need to do that as well."

Chapter 7

Blaze walked through his home the next morning, his phone to his ear. The call was not what he wanted to hear. There were two children missing and his charity had been approached for help. Only, there was not a lot of information forthcoming. Blaze knew his staff was working to determine if this was a legitimate call or a prank call. Those were common. There had been an interview and investigative process set up that was adhered to rigorously.

"What have you discovered, Stu?" Blaze sat at his desk, reaching for a pen. "That bad? Okay. Talk to the police and find out what you can. You know the drill." Blaze set his phone to one side. This call to his office had been bizarre, he decided. There just didn't seem to be enough information available. He thought that it was a fishing call and Stu would confirm if it was or not.

Blaze dropped down in his desk chair, his phone set to one side as he reached to pull up his email program. He was lost in his work shortly, not seeing Bevin as she hesitated at the doorway, watching him, before moving on.

Bevin was at a loss. She needed to be at her work. Only she had quit that job and been on the run, she gathered, for the last few days. Bevin had no idea what she was to do, turning as she felt an arm around her. Mary stood there, watching Bevin and then Blaze. Blaze, she knew, would be working for a while, lost to those around him.   He didn't realize that he was Bevin's lifeline at the present time.

Turning away from the front of the cabin, Bevin walked away. She felt too dangerous to stay, yet she also felt it too dangerous to leave. She just didn't realize the consternation that would happen by walking away.

Mary tapped at the office door thirty minutes after Bevin had left. She had gone looking for her. Only she couldn't find her. She saw Blaze's head raise as he looked up before he was on his feet.

"Mary?   You had a question?"   Blaze had momentarily forgotten about his house guest.

"It's Bevin. I can't find her anywhere. I think that she's left." Mary was distraught. She had liked Bevin from the first moment that she met her. To have her disappear was not what she wanted.

"Bevin? She's gone?" Blaze stared past Mary before he was moving towards the door. He searched outside before he stood staring at the road and then running for his vehicle.

Driving slowly along the road, Blaze searched for Bevin. He knew that it had only been about thirty minutes since Mary had seen Bevin but that was long enough for her to have disappeared. Blaze didn't want that. He didn't want Bevin to disappear at all from his life, he decided. Just why that was, he couldn't have said at that moment.

Blaze pulled to a stop, his eyes on the figure sitting under a tree. It was Bevin. She had not really

---

gotten that far from his home but it was far enough that she could have disappeared. Out of the vehicle, Blaze approached her and then just sat at her side, not feeling that words were even necessary at that point.

Bevin stared at Blaze before she lowered her head. He just had to follow her. She had been praying for someone to come along and give her a lift into town. Blaze was not who she had been praying for. Obviously, God thought differently than she did.

"Go home, Blaze." Bevin's voice was low and angry. She wasn't angry at Blaze. She was angry at life in general even though she had to acknowledge that God was in control and that He knew best what was His plan for her.

"No, I don't think so, Bevin. You worried Mary and that worried me. Come back with me." Blaze waited patiently for Bevin to decide. If she didn't decide soon, he would just gather her up and take her back to his home.

"I can't, Blaze. I'm too dangerous." Bevin was sorrowful as she spoke, sure that she was a dangerous person to know.

"We don't know that for sure, Bevin. Come. Let's go home. I'm sorry that I got lost in my work but we had some situations that had to be dealt with." Blaze simply extended his hand and waited for Bevin to react. His prayer for her was that she would be protected.

"Where is God, Blaze? He can't be allowing this to happen." Bevin almost spat her words at Blaze.

—

"He is right here, Bevin. He has never left you and never will. He only wants the best for you. Sometimes, though, His best means danger and difficulty for us. He covers us with His hand and shelters us. Sometimes, too, His best means that He allows us to be hurt or even die. It is how His will works." Blaze didn't look at her. He simply prayed for her.

Bevin had turned to study him before she sighed. Her hand reached for that of Blaze, finding his tightening on hers. She was conflicted, wanting to run but also wanting to stay with this tall handsome man who seemed to be trying to take care of her. She hadn't had that in a long time, she decided.

"How do we do this, Blaze? How do we continue to live our lives without knowing who is out there and means us harm?"

"I don't know exactly, Bevin. But we walk forward with our confidence in God. He is the One who has already walked this path." He was on his feet, drawing her up to hers and then into a hug. Bevin was shocked, to say the least. She was not a hugger but had found out over the last few hours that Blaze was.

"I guess, then, Blaze, I go back with you. But I need to find something to do." Bevin blinked back tears. She felt wanted, cherished, adored, and loved by Blaze, if that was even possible. She didn't think it was, not on such short notice.

"We'll find something for you to do. Mary has a charity that she runs, looking out for children who need tutoring. Talk to her. It may be something that you can help with in the background. She doesn't have enough time to sort through all the material that she wants to use." Blaze slipped behind the steering wheel and then turned the vehicle around. "Let's go home, Bevin. You can speak with her. And I am done with what I need to for the moment. If something urgent comes up, my secretary will reach out to me."

Bevin stared at him in shock. Here he was, solving problems for her.

"Is that what it is, Blaze? Home?"

Chapter 8

Frank stood and watched the younger couple as they faced off against one another. Blaze had come to find Bevin, determined to decide for her what she wanted to do. Bevin was just as determined that she needed to leave because she had brought danger to him. Frank rubbed at his upper lip, trying hard to conceal the smile that he just couldn't conceal. He had no idea which one of them would ultimately win. He walked forward, his portfolio dropped on the kitchen table as he reached to pour himself a cup of coffee. He was a frequent enough visitor, either on personal or police business, that he felt comfortable doing that.

Bevin's eyes broke contact with Blaze for a moment as she frowned at Frank. He had been around and taken their statements. She just didn't know why he was back again. Bevin turned towards the back door of the kitchen, her hand reaching for the lever handle to escape the room, before Blaze simply wrapped her into his arms and drew her back against himself, holding her just tightly enough that she was unable to escape despite her struggles.

"Let me go, Blaze." Bevin was scared, if truth must be told. She didn't like dealing with the police, the police in her hometown notorious for harassing the ladies no matter the age.

"It's okay, Bevin. Frank just needs to go over some things with us. It's what he does." Blaze finally managed to calm the lady in his arms and help her to a seat at the kitchen table. He rested a hand on her shoulder for a moment before he placed a mug of coffee in front of her. His mug hit the table beside hers as he pulled back that chair and sat. Blaze then reached for her hand, feeling her tugging at hers but not letting go. "Frank? You're here for a reason?"

"I am, Blaze. First, we need to pray." Frank's head was bowed as he did just that, Blaze's voice picking up the petition when he finished.

Bevin had stared at Frank for a moment, not sure if this was really happening. The officers that she knew were more apt to use God's name as a curse word rather than the way these two men were using it. She looked at Frank as his head raised, seeing that he was uncertain how to proceed. Bevin sighed. There had to be an answer out there somewhere that would solve what she was going through and then she could be on her way to another town. Only, she didn't want that any more. She just wanted to stay where Blaze was.

Blaze kept his gaze on Bevin, seeing how torn that she was. He knew right well that she would run if given the opportunity. He was not prepared to give her that and he knew that Frank would do what he could to prevent it, to the point of arresting her as a material witness to an unsolved crime. That said crime would be solved, Blaze knew. He just didn't know how long it would take or how much danger that Bevin was in. He didn't look at himself as being in danger. That was a fact of life for him.

"Frank? What do you need to tell us or ask us?" Blaze looked over at the man whom he considered a friend.

"Good question, Blaze. I do have some questions but first, Bevin? Tell me about your life. We spoke briefly the other day when I got your statement. I need to understand why you kept moving from town to town." He waited patiently as Bevin rubbed at the wooden table top, her eyes on her hand.

"What can I tell you? I just didn't fit into the towns where I ended up. Something kept pushing me to move. Mom and Dad didn't like it. They wanted me to stay in my hometown. I couldn't. I hate it. There was no freedom in being a lady there unless you were married and even then, that didn't always work. The police harassed any single lady there until they either married or left town. I wasn't prepared to marry anyone there. I ended up leaving for college and then never went back, not even to visit. My parents always came to where I was living."

Frank nodded. He knew her hometown and what the atmosphere for living there was like. He didn't blame her one bit for leaving. Frank's chief had spoken in depth with Frank. At this point, he had spoken to another force and asked for a review of that town's police force. Neither officer expected it to be a good review, not from what they were hearing. Bevin was not the first one to complain about that force. They both thought, however, that someone was going after her and that person belonged to that force in some way.

"That's what I thought. Just so you know, we have received some complaints about the police force there. My chief of police has asked another force to investigate." Frank's hand went up. "You are not the

---

complainant in this case, Bevin. They may come after you. That's part of the reason we need you to stay here. Blaze is fine with you staying here as are we. He has really good security and with Mary and Art here on site all the time, there is no question about your reputation. If you leave town and move to another town or even move into town, then you are vulnerable and may be injured or killed. We would like to prevent that if at all possible." Frank smiled at the shocked look on her face.

"An investigation? After all this time? I don't know what to say." Bevin's hand tightened on Blaze. She knew full well how much danger she would be in. There were things about her town that she knew that she would never tell anyone. Then, Bevin sighed. "What do you need to know about them?"

Frank gave her a smile, kindness on his face. Bevin was reacting how he had prayed that she would. He just hadn't been sure that she would.

"For now? Nothing. The chief will want to speak with you or have me take the information that you can give and we'll pass it on. The investigation is just in the preliminary stages. We will do everything that we can to protect you, Bevin. That is our promise and a commitment to our residents that we take very deeply. You are a resident here for now. I would like you to stay here. You are searching for somewhere to live where you will feel welcome and at home, aren't you?"

Bevin looked up at Blaze, seeing a look in his eyes that said he prayed and hoped that she would never leave Grasspoint and never leave him. She frowned at him for a moment before he grinned at her. This couldn't be right, she thought. We don't know each other enough to make that kind of commitment. At least, I don't think that we do. God, is this You? Did You bring me here?

"I guess for now, I'll stay. What about those men?" Bevin's gaze went back to Frank, seeing the soft yellows of the wall behind him.

"Those men? They have been transferred to another jurisdiction where they are wanted for murder." Frank watched Bevin's face pale. "We don't know if that was their plan for you or not or even who sent them after you. That is something that we need to determine. Right now? You need to stay safe. How do we do that? You'll want to be out and about, Bevin."

"I do. I need to get to town for some purchases if I am to stay here. This is hard." Bevin swiped at the tears on her face, feeling Blaze's arm come around her and hug her to him. "Other than you two, Mary, and Art, I don't know anyone here. And that hurts."

"It does, sweetheart." Blaze kept his eyes on Frank who was nodding. "We have some friends who would be willing to speak with you. They went through what we term as adventures similar to what you seem to be off on."

Bevin turned her head, finding herself almost nose to nose with Blaze. That didn't startle her or upset her. She could feel his caring and compassion in how he was hugging her.

"You do? And they would?" Her head turned as Frank gave a laugh. "Frank?"

"They would. A lady by the name of Ashlynn and her four nieces, Brinn, Chani, Darbi, and Eilis. How be Sue and I come your way on Sunday, Blaze, and bring the ladies and their families with us?"

"That sounds like a plan, Frank. I know without asking that they would be willing to speak with Bevin. Darbi in fact sent me a text this morning, asking me what kind of adventure I was on and if they could speak with the lady involved." His finger on Bevin's lips stopped any protest. "I have not said anything, sweetheart. It's just how intuitive that these ladies are."

Chapter 9

Blaze walked Bevin towards an exclusive woman's shop, much to her protest. She couldn't afford to shop there, she told him. She only had limited funds. Blaze had simply grinned and told her not to worry. That one of his charities would pick up the charges for her clothes. He wanted her to do this for him. If she was really adamant that she wouldn't, then Blaze would take her elsewhere. Blaze had prayed for years for a lady of his own to shop there and here she was. He had already determined that she was his lady. He just needed to wait for her to decide that she was his.

Annie, the owner of the store, stared in shock as Blaze entered, Bevin's hand tight in his. She had never seen him hold a lady's hand and she had been a friend all of their lives.

"Blaze? Who do we have here?" Annie reached to hug her friend and then surprised Bevin by hugging her.

"This is Bevin Connors. She's the unfortunate victim of losing all of her clothing and whatnot when her car disappeared. Can you help her?" Blaze nodded at Bevin who by this time had turned to study the clothing. Blaze beckoned Annie to one side. "This is not going through the charity, Annie. I'm personally taking care of this." Bevin refused to acknowledge the question on Annie's face. Any acknowledgement of his feelings had to go to Bevin first.

Blaze stepped outside the shop, knowing that Annie would do what she did best and find the articles of clothing that Bevin would likely protest at. He eyed the store next door and sighed. It was too early in their friendship to buy any jewelry for Bevin as much as he wanted to. His eyes then raised as he felt watched, finding a man standing across the street with his eyes on Blaze. Blaze simply raised his phone, took a photo, and sent it on to Frank. Frank he knew would deal with the man. This had to be what the Whitman ladies had meant, he decided, about being monitored and followed.

Bevin turned towards Blaze an hour later, distress on her face. He simply hugged her, took the bags that Annie was extending towards him, a quiet thank you to his friend, and then turned Bevin to the door. The bags were tucked into the back of his SUV before his hands rested on Bevin's shoulders.

"It's okay to be upset and angry and sad, Bevin. Those are all emotions that are normal. As I said, you are not responsible for what happened. Whoever is after you? They are. For now, you're staying with me. I spoke with your father last night. He called."

"He did? He wanted to speak with you. I wasn't sure if he would have reached out to you yet or not." Bevin sighed, her head going down against Blaze's arm. He had taken her hand and was not letting go of her. "How much trouble am I in?"

Blaze grinned at the plaintive tone in her voice, his eyes following a man walking towards him. He turned them abruptly into a store and walked through it, waving at the store owner, who simply nodded at

Blaze. Blaze shoved open the employees' only door and then stopped, drawing Bevin close to him for a moment before he looked around and headed for the outside door. His hand rested on it for a moment before he withdrew it. There was just no way that he could open the door.

Bevin frowned at him before pointing at the door. Blaze shook his head, knowing that he would not walk out of it. He couldn't. God had stopped him and he had learned early in life to obey when God spoke. His finger on her lips kept her silent. Stepping back to the inside door, Blaze looked around, tugging Bevin into a tight spot behind some boxes. Wrapping her into his arms, he simply waited.

The interior door flew open violently even as the store owner protested. The couple could hear the rapid footsteps of the two men who had been tracking them. The sound of the outside door flying open came to them. Blaze waited, not willing to put them out there yet.

The store owner had angrily followed the men, snapping on the lock to the back door before moving to the front door. A patrol officer had appeared, seeing the commotion at the back door as the men hammered at it to get back in. A quick conversation with the owner had the officer heading for the back of the store and arresting the men. Their protest was very loud and clear but it made no difference. All the officers in town moved in to help Blaze and particularly at this time when he was under attack. Blaze supported the officers in more ways than one and this was little that they could do to repay him.

—

Bevin finally shoved away from Blaze, his arms dropping to his sides, as she headed back into the store. She was angry, not at Blaze, but at the circumstances that had just occurred.

Blaze followed her, a slight smile on his face despite the fear that had rushed through him. He had been certain that they would be found and that Bevin would disappear on him. He didn't know if his heart could take that. He had acknowledged to himself in the wee hours of the morning that he did love Bevin. He just had to convince her to stay so that he could court her.

"Bevin? It's not his fault." Blaze wrapped his arms around her, stopping her in her tracks.

Bevin stood still, her eyes slightly closed. No, she decided, it was not the store owner's fault. It was the fault of whoever it was that was after either her or Blaze. That was what she couldn't decide or understand.

"Are we safe to leave, Blaze?" She leaned back against him, feeling his strength in how he gently held her.

"I would think so." Blaze looked up to see Frank walking their way. "And here's Frank."

"Blaze? Bevin? Do you two know how close you two were to disappearing again?" Frank was angry and it showed in the tone of his voice.

"I would think so, Frank, seeing as we had to run and hide." Blaze shook his head at his friend. "We'll talk, Frank. For now, take our statements and then I think we need to head for home."

"We'll do that. Where are you parked?" Frank had seen Blaze's SUV and at the moment had an officer searching it to find anything that didn't belong.

"Right outside. You well know which is my vehicle." Blaze's own anger was flaring, driven in part by his fear for his lady.

"I know. Now, tell me what happened." Frank listened carefully, realizing that neither one of the couple knew who the men were. And that concerned him. Someone was after his friend and the lady who had appeared in his life. And no one knew who had hired those men or the reason why.

Chapter 10

Blaze paced his home office that afternoon. He had returned to that room, despite wanting to be where Bevin was. She had simply taken all the bags and headed for the bedroom that she was using. He didn't hear the low sobs or see the tears that were streaking down her face. Mary had and had simply followed Blaze's lady to hug her.

He turned as he heard footsteps and sighed. Frank and George were there. Now what, he wondered? Where did it end?

"Frank? George? You're here?" Blaze sank into his desk chair, knowing that he wouldn't be finding Bevin at any point soon.

"We are, Blaze. This morning? What caused you to run?" Frank went right to the point.

"I saw the one man watching us. I was hoping to take Bevin out the back door but God stopped me. We hid. Fred's okay?"

"He is. Fred is just very worried about you." Frank acknowledged that question. "Did you know that man you saw?"

Blaze shook his head. He had a good memory for faces.

"I've never seen him before. How is he connected to the other two men?"

"He's not saying but he is wanted here for multiple charges and also in other jurisdictions."

George spoke up. "Do you know how close you two were?"

"We know exactly how close we were. Now, what are you doing about it?" Bevin had appeared, coming to ask Blaze a question, a question that died on her lips as she heard the conversation between the men.

Blaze was on his feet, drawing Bevin into the room and to a chair that he pulled close to his own chair. He shoved her down into it, reaching for her hand. He could feel her fingers tightening on his.

"I am sure that you do." Frank eyed her, seeing the anger and resignation on her face. "Have you thought of any reason for you being chased from town to town?"

Bevin frowned at him, trying to understand what he was asking.

"I'm not sure I know what you mean." Bevin was refusing to back down, having been scared that day and wanting to know why.

"We've gone back over all the towns that you have lived in, spoken to your employers and your work mates and even your landlords. It is common with all of them to state that you seemed to be on the run but none of them could tell us why." Frank watched her more closely.

"I was, I guess. I just thought I was restless." Bevin leaned her head against Blaze's arm, seeking comfort from her contact with him.

"No, you weren't restless, Bevin." George looked up from his notes, sharing a look with Frank.

—

54

"You were being chased and chased to this town. We need to understand why so that we can find the men or women responsible. Someone from outside our town would not have known that building was Blaze's but from what we can determine, you were chased there and then the confrontation happened just as Blaze was exiting the building."

"It was a setup?" Blaze commented, a sigh coming from him. "That means we need to go back over all the threats I've received."

"We're doing that, Blaze. You have always been honest with us and forwarded any to us. But it may be that this is a new threat and one that you have never received before. That is our thinking." Frank could only be honest with the man sitting in front of him. He watched as Blaze's arm came around Bevin and hugged her to himself. He gave a half-smile. Just like the others who had had these types of adventures, Blaze had found his lady. God had led there, Frank decided, but it would be God who protected Blaze and Bevin. This seemed to be out of human control for the moment.

"I am sure that you are. I just don't understand why me and why Bevin." Blaze looked down at the lady in his arms. "We have never met, not that I am aware of. Bevin had no idea what I do for a living until it was explained to her. So, how did whoever it is connect us?"

"That we are working on, Blaze. Information is slow in coming in. I have gone to Garrett, Gareth's father, and also to Emma Finlay. They are working on it but are finding they are reaching roadblocks."

Frank's attention went to George for a moment before he turned to Bevin. "I have reached out to both sets of parents. They're trying to come up with names or events but once more, neither are certain that they have ever met or even been in the same area at the same time. It could just be a chance encounter or passing or having them at the same event or conference that has connected you two."

Blaze nodded. That had been his thought, that somehow their parents had connected and for whatever reason, the person or persons who were causing all this turmoil had connected Bevin and himself.

"I would think it would be that, Frank. Bevin tells me her parents are flying in today. Mom and Dad will be around later. We'll talk with them." Blaze's hand went up. "I know that you need to in an official capacity. For today, we meet with our parents. It will be hard enough on Bevin to do that."

Blaze was on his feet to walk Frank and George out.

"What are the chances of Bevin speaking with Ashlynn or her girls?" Blaze was friends with them. He was just hesitant to ask for that.

"I'll speak with them, Blaze. I have no doubt that they would be willing to do that. You're good friends with the girls, particularly Darbi. I'll get back to you on that." Frank walked away with George, frustrated that they were no further ahead in what they needed to find.

Bevin hesitated as she came to find Blaze, surprised to find him simply gathering her close to his side and then walking them down the steps and around to the back where he found seats in an area surrounded by perennial flowers. His head went back for a moment as his eyes closed.

"Blaze? What are we to do? I can't stay here. I'm too dangerous for you to be around." Bevin was working herself into a frenzy, her words choppy and short.

"You stay here, Bevin. I don't want you to leave, ever." Blaze didn't hear the words that he had spoken, putting his heart out there. His eyes searched the face of the lady who he still held in his arms.

Bevin stilled in her movements, hearing Blaze's words. She turned to him, a puzzled yet hopeful look on her face.

"Blaze? Did you mean that?" Bevin waited for him to think through his words.

"Mean what, sweetheart?" Blaze really couldn't remember what he had said.

"That you didn't want me to ever leave?" Bevin watched as his eyes slid closed and her heart dropped. He didn't mean then after all.

Blaze hugged her tighter, a kiss to her forehead. He could feel her relaxing against him.

"I did, Bevin. I don't want you to leave me, ever. God has brought the lady that He meant for me into my life. I am so afraid that you will walk away from me or be hurt or even killed." He didn't look at her, not wanting to see her refusal to believe him or God on her face.

—

Bevin stared at him and then twisted enough that she could hug him. God, this is You. You have brought the knight into my life who was prayed for.

"Thank you, Bevin. I won't leave. Not unless God tells me to. Right now? He's saying to stay. But what do we do?" Bevin was conflicted to say the least. She didn't want to stay and bring more harm to Blaze but at the same time, he made her feel safe and secure as well as cherished, added and loved.

Chapter 11

Running for his vehicle the next day, Blaze dodged the raindrops that were slowly falling. He had had to be in his office, not by choice at the time, but from necessity. Missing children didn't wait for someone to decide that they were important. It was always a priority with Blaze and his staff to immediately reach out to whatever law enforcement entity needed to be involved. This time, it was a young boy who had gone missing. Time was of an essence as always,

Sliding behind the wheel, Blaze hesitated for a moment before he keyed the vehicle to life. Something seemed off about that request to find the boy, almost as if it was a fishing expedition from someone trying to trap him. His staff had felt the same way.

An incoming call had Blaze pulling to the side of the road. He frowned as he listened to his second-in-comnmand, a man who had been with his father for years and then began to work with Blaze when Blaze took over the charity work.

"So, it was a set up." Blaze sighed. "And you've passed everything on."

"I have, Blaze." Timothy Steele nodded at Frank who was sitting across from him at a table in a conference room in the building. "Frank is here. We both think that it was to try and force you out into the open. No one should have the information that this person had. I hate to think that we might have a leak somewhere here."

"We might. Look at the new hires in that area and then work your way up. Contact Emma at Trackers and give her all the names and everything that she needs. She'll make it a priority for us if she can." Blaze sat for a moment after the call dropped before he shook his head. This was not making sense. They had never had this in all the years that the charity had been in operation. So what made it different at this point? The only new thing or person in his life was Bevin, and he refused to believe that she had anything to do with that.

Bevin turned as she heard footsteps behind her, finding herself wrapped into a hug. Blaze had found her before he had done anything other than arrive home. He had needed to reassure himself that Bevin was still there and hadn't fled to some town where he couldn't find her and where she would be in more danger.

"Blaze? What happened today?" Bevin struggled to release herself from Blaze's hug, just not able to do that.

"Someone tried to scam us with a missing child. It wasn't the case. So, now we have to have someone look into everyone in that unit." Blaze was frustrated to say the least. God had protected them all these years and now this.

"They did? That's odd. How does it go with what we're going through? Or does it?" Bevin finally managed to escape from his hug and paced. "What do we do now?"

"We don't do anything." Blaze's hand went up as her mouth opened to protest. "It's okay. I have a friend who will look into it for us. And now, what have you been up to today?" He grinned as she stared at him, her mouth opening and closing.

"What have I been up to? Not a lot. I don't like being idle, Blaze. It's not me. But there doesn't seem to be much that I can do." Bevin was frustrated. She had spoken with her mother, who simply told her that they were delayed in flying out and they didn't know why. "Mom and Dad have not flown out yet. They're delayed and don't know why." Bevin paled as she thought through what that could mean. "Someone's keeping them away from me."

Blaze had had that thought and had sent his company plane and pilot out to find them and bring them home.

"I thought of that. Terry, the company pilot, is out there. He'll connect with them and then bring them back. That way, they're not in danger on a flight or between flights." Blaze reached to hug her again. "We'll get them here and safely, sweetheart. You need them and they need you."

"Thank you, Blaze. This is costing you an awful lot. I'll never be able to repay you." Bevin swiped at the tears on her face. She had not heard the older couple who had entered the room and then stopped at a motion from Blaze's hand.

"I would never charge a friend to help them. It's not who I am or what I do. You're important to me, Bevin. And that means I want to do everything I can to help you. Frank talked to me earlier today and was hoping to be by here this afternoon to speak with you. They are no further ahead right now. Anyone who has been arrested has been transferred to another jurisdiction and didn't speak before they left. We'll work it as well. I reached out to Emma, a friend who finds people and places that no one else can. She'll be back to us within a day with what she has found if she can." He turned her to face his parents. "Right now, my parents are here and would very much like to meet you."

Bevin stared up at him, not sure if he was telling her to truth. A soft sound had her staring ahead at the couple who had approached. She could see the resemblance to Blaze in his father.

"Hi! I think I'm the one causing all the trouble." Bevin's voice was subdued. She was ready to run and run as far and as hard as she could, thinking that she would be blamed for Blaze disappearing and facing danger.

Brody and Emily Framer shared a look before Emily simply moved in on Bevin to hug her. She felt the younger lady holding on to her, needing contact with a mother when hers wasn't around. Brody had hugged his son and then stood with an arm around Blaze's shoulders, his keen eyes searching his son's face before he nodded. It was as they had suspected. Blaze had found his lady but wasn't quite sure if his lady had found her knight or not.

Brody nudged Emily aside after a couple of moments so that he could hug Bevin as well. A father's prayer was whispered in her ears, causing her to blink rapidly to clear away more tears.

"Welcome to our family, Bevin." Brody stood back at last, his arm around his wife. "Now, what are we up to right now? Researching your adventure, Blaze?" He grinned at his son, causing Bevin to frown at him.

"Researching it? How would we be able to do that?" Bevin was confused. They were police investigators or even private investigators.

"We are able to do that, sweetheart." Blaze turned her from the office and towards the kitchen. "We'll have our dinner and then work on it. Terry has sent a text message. He connected with your parents, gathered up their belongings, and is in the air heading here. They'll be here sometime in the early morning hours." He found himself the recipient of a quick hug before Bevin moved away with Emily.

Brody studied his son for a moment.

"She's your heart, isn't she, son?" Brody didn't wait for an answer. He knew his son well enough to be able to read him.

Blaze stared after his father before his eyes closed. God had provided the lady who was his heart. Right now, all he could do was pray for her and her protection. He knew that God was in control. It was just difficult not to jump in and smother Bevin. That was something that she would not allow.

Chapter 12

Frank dropped his portfolio on the coffee table in Blaze's home office before he headed for the kitchen. He had been on the run all day and the offer of a meal had been welcome. He greeted Brody and Emily, friends for years before he turned to Blaze and then Bevin. Frank frowned. Something was up with Bevin. He didn't know her well enough to read her but his instincts were telling him that she was hiding something and he wanted to know what.

"Bevin? What did you remember?" That was Frank's first question directed at her as they gathered back in the office. Their meal had been shared as had a time of prayer.

Bevin shrugged. Her thoughts were muddled, not at all the clear way that she thought.

"I don't know, Frank. I am getting bits and pieces of things that happened in the towns that I lived in. Not enough to know what happened but enough that it scares me." Bevin reached for a notebook where she had been jotting down her thoughts. "Here. This is what I have. I'm sorry that it isn't in any concise and orderly manner." She felt Blaze's arm around her, tucking her close to him. She frowned at him. He kept doing that, she knew, and it did make her feel safe. But she would be moving on when this was all over, no matter if it was her or Blaze who had been the targeted victim.

Frank nodded as he accepted the book and began to read through it. On his feet, he headed to make a copy of it, handing Bevin back the original.

"You keep this, Bevin. I have copies if that is okay with you to work from. Continue to write what you can and let me have copies of that. It may well be what triggers something and solves this." Frank smiled as she shook her head. "You don't think so."

"No, I don't. I don't know if it's me or Blaze that are the targets. And you can't tell us that, can you?" Bevin waited for Frank to respond.

"No, I can't tell you that, Bevin. We're not that far along in the investigation to know that." Frank paused for a moment. "We did find your car."

"You did? When can I get it?" Bevin frowned as Frank continued to shake his head. "Frank? My car?"

"I'm sorry, Bevin. It was burnt. We weren't able to remove anything of yours from it. This was done on purpose to drive you away from safety." Frank was on his feet, heading for the door, his phone in his hand. An urgent call had come in that he had to take whether he wanted to or not.

Bevin blinked in horror and then fear at the thought of something destroying her car and then destroying what life she had in her things. Thankfully, anything really important was still at her family home. It just distressed her that someone would go to these lengths to destroy her life.

—

Blaze tightened his hold on his lady, his eyes on his father. Brody was nodding. He had suspected that this was what had happened to Bevin's car. He had already reached out to one of their charities about replacing the vehicle. He knew that Blaze had already replaced her clothing, much to her distress and under protest.

"Bevin? May I see what you have written?" Brody waited patiently for Bevin to respond. He took the proffered notebook, glancing through it before he too was on his feet to make a copy. He handed her back the book just as Frank had and then reached for pens and markers. He was soon lost in his reading, Emily shaking her head at Bevin.

"He'll read it through many times, Bevin, making notes and highlighting what he needs to. Then he'll speak with you. For now, your parents will be staying here for a couple of days, I would imagine. If you will, come with me and we'll figure out which room is best for them." Emily was on her feet, her arm around the younger lady who seemed reluctant to walk away from Blaze.

Blaze stood, a bemused look on his face, as Bevin looked back at him before the two ladies disappeared from sight. He loved her, he knew. He just didn't know if she would love him back.

"Dad?" Blaze waited for his father to look up. "How do we do this?"

"How do we do what? Keep you two safe?" At Blaze's nod, Brody set the paperwork to one side. He had always listened to his son, setting aside whatever it was he was involved in, if possible, to do just that. "We can make all sorts of plans, Blaze, but we may not be able to use them. We'll talk to Abe, Richard, and Don as well to see what their thoughts are. Frank will have some ideas as well. He's to be around later, isn't he?"

"He is. I don't like what happened, Dad. Somewhere there's a leak or someone has spoken out of turn. I want to know who. This has placed our work in jeopardy." Blaze was on his feet, moving away from his father and towards where he could hear his mother, Mary, and Bevin. He stopped where he could watch Bevin without being seen.

Bevin was trying hard to relax but just not able to. She felt threatened and chased. She also worried about bringing danger to Blaze and his family. Bevin looked up at that point to find Blaze watching her, his emotions open on his face. His love for her, already there in his heart, was on his face as well. Bevin drew in a deep breath and without excusing herself from the ladies walked towards him, following him as he backed away. She stopped in the entrance to the living room, her eyes searching the comfortable room. Bevin liked the soft colours that Blaze had chosen and the comfortable furniture. A fire was lit in the fireplace to distill the dampness from outside. It was a room that she could live in, she decided, for the rest of her life. Only that wasn't about to happen.

"Blaze?" Bevin kept her voice low, not wanting to draw any attention to them.

—

"Bevin? Are you okay?" Blaze approached her, his hands out for hers. He watched as she hesitated a moment before her hands were in his.

"I don't know, Blaze. I really don't. I have no idea how I am to feel at this point. I need to be working but I don't know what to do. I had quit my employment in the last town and was going to seek something else. Only I was chased from there and life got in the way." Her voice was sober as she spoke.

"I know, sweetheart. I know." Blaze reached to wrap her into a hug, finding her hugging him in return. "What can we do that will keep you safe? I don't want to lose you. No one else does either." His eyes were on the entrance to the living room, seeing Frank waiting there, not entering until Blaze nodded. "Frank's here, sweetheart."

"He is? Has he solved this yet?" Bevin slipped away from Blaze to almost run to the other end of the room where she spun to stare at Frank.

Frank watched her, an amused look peeking out of his eyes. She was ready to run and that was a problem. If she ran, she would end up in the hands of the men after her and would disappear. That was the word that had reached to George that morning. And none of them wanted that for her.

Chapter 13

Frank dropped his portfolio on the coffee table, turning away from Bevin for a moment. He shared a look with Blaze, a frown on his face for a moment before it cleared. It was obvious that Blaze had feelings for Bevin. Anyone who knew him well could tell. Blaze usually kept his emotions hidden. Today, he was not doing that.

"Blaze? Bevin? We need to talk and talk now. Abe is on his way in as is Richard and Don." Frank was not backing away from the couple. "We need to make plans. I know, Blaze. You have plans in place with your security team. And we welcome those. But this is different. This involves something outside of your work, as far as we can tell, and it involves Bevin."

"It does." Blaze sighed before he walked towards Bevin, simply reaching for her hand and tugging her over to a couch. Sitting, he pulled her down with him and then wrapped her close to him.

Bevin was shocked when he did that and struggled for a moment before she just gave up trying to move away from him. He wasn't allowing her to do that. Her attention went to Frank even though her thoughts were with her parents. She needed them right at that moment and they weren't there. Bevin was grateful that Blaze had reached out to them and was flying them home. It didn't solve the problem of missing them however.

"Frank? What can you tell us?" Blaze broke the silence in the room, watching his friend closely.

—

"What can I tell you? Not a lot at present, Blaze. This person who contacted you about the missing child? He's disappeared. The phone number turned out to be a fake. Now, what do we do about that?" Frank was angry at this person, knowing full well that if a child had been lost or exploited, Blaze would have been out there. "We believe that this was a deliberate attempt to draw you out and away from your security."

Blaze nodded. That was what he had expected Frank to say.

"Now what? Where do we go from here? I can work from home most day, doing video conferencing as I need to, but I still have to be at the office at least one day a week." Blaze turned his attention to Bevin, finding her with her gaze fixed on Frank. "And where does that leave Bevin? Are we any closer to finding out who is after her or why?"

"We're not, Blaze. That is concerning, of course. If we don't know, we can't protect Bevin." Frank's hand went up at her protest. "We want to protect you, Bevin. We don't like it in this town when ladies are threatened. And that is exactly what happened to you. I know that you have been honest with us and we appreciate that. We also understand the frustration that you feel, not being able to have the freedom to move around as you wish. Our people are watching out for you, even the ones on the street. That's what we do." Frank left shortly afterwards, frustrated at not being able to solve this mystery or end whatever this adventure was.

"What do we do now?" Bevin made no effort to move away from Blaze, content to be held. Blaze didn't think that she realized he still had her wrapped in his arms.

"I don't know, sweetheart. I really don't. Frank is working it as best he can with the limited information that he has. Emma, the friend I mentioned, is working it as well but has hit roadblocks that she usually doesn't. She did say that she would be calling to speak with you at some point, unless she and Abe show up here in person. And they might. Abe has a security team and would be a good resource for you to speak with."

"Do I know these people?" Bevin didn't think that she did even though the names seemed familiar.

"I don't know if you would. I do just because of what has gone on in the past." Blaze was on his feet, needing to do something. "Come on, sweetheart. Let's see what we need to do for dinner. I think Mom was wanting me to grill."

Bevin stared at him, not sure what he was up to but feeling loved and cherished in just how he treated her.

"You know, you don't act as if you had millions of dollars." She smirked as he turned to stare at her.

"I don't? No, I guess that I don't. We don't look at it as if it were our money. It's God's money and we are just the stewards for it. Using it as we do? That is how we are trying to be the hands and feet for God on earth." Blaze sighed. Not many people understood what they said when they said that.

———

Bevin nodded, having come to that conclusion herself.

"It is how you are working and serving Him. And we serve an awesome God. We just don't like what we have to go through sometimes. Like this with us now. We don't understand the why's of what we're facing or who it is. That's something we need to work on." Bevin was adamant that she was not sitting back and not trying to figure out who it was.

"We can do that." Blaze groaned as his phone chimed. It was his personal one, not his work one. That one was sitting on his desk. He peered at the message and then hugged Bevin, startling her.

"Blaze? What on earth? What are you doing?" Bevin shoved away from him, a question on her face.

"Sorry. It's Terry. He's heard from our pilot. He's made good time and is landing shortly on our runway. That means your parents are almost here." Blaze grinned at her as she stared at him and then hugged him. "I take it this is good news?"

"It is, Blaze. Very good news. But where will they stay? I need to make arrangements for them." Bevin walked away from him to stand staring out of the living room window, her teeth worrying at her bottom lip. She didn't know this town and had no idea where to begin to them a place to stay.

Blaze approached her, his hands gently placed on her shoulders. He felt her jump as he did so.

"It's okay, sweetheart. We have lots of room here for them to stay. We also have a cabin just ten minutes from here that they are welcome to use if they want to. We will not separate you from them. You need them here and they need to be with you." Blaze walked away at that point, not realizing that he had dropped a kiss on her cheek.

Bevin's hand found her cheek, surprise on her face as she spun to watch him leave. What had he meant by that, she wondered? It was not in his character to go around kissing ladies. Her face softened as she thought it through. Was he the knight in her bedtime stories, the one that she had been searching for? It had to be God who brought them together, she decided. It wasn't them. She had had no plans of running to his building that day but it had been the only place where she had decided to seek refuge. She just hadn't made it to the actual building but Blaze had stepped in and rescued her.

Blaze stopped and stared back at Bevin, watching her search for him. He gave a sad smile. He knew that they were in danger and once it was over, she would disappear. All he could do was petition his Heavenly Father to protect her in all manners. He just wasn't sure how he could do that on his own. Friends were contacting him, wanting to help. At some point, he would meet with them and Bevin and decide from there what they needed to do. And he was afraid that Bevin would just take off and run, particularly with her parents near her.

Brody approached his son, a piece of paper in his hand and a question on his lips. Instead, he stood beside his son, grown so tall, an arm across Blaze's shoulders as he prayed for his son. He was afraid,

—

73

knowing the character of those after Blaze and Bevin. He didn't know why, but he was troubled at what information was being forwarded to him. And that information? Brody needed to go over it with both Blaze and Bevin. He just didn't know when that would happen or if the danger creeping closer to the younger couple would take them away from the families again.

———

Chapter 14

Brody watched his son closely that night. Blaze was distraught, he could tell, but was refusing to speak with his father. He had no way of knowing how to get him to do just that. Blaze's attention seemed to be just on Bevin. That was unusual for his son. Brody walked away to the outside and to stalk around the cabin and garage. Someone was out there, he knew, watching for his son to appear. If that happened, Brody was afraid that Blaze would disappear and if Bevin was with him, so would she. He didn't know if he could handle that again after having the couple disappear already.

Not hearing the running footsteps, Brody didn't see the man who had approached and then tackled him to the ground. He tried to fight back but a single blow to his temple sent him spiralling down into darkness. The man sat back on his heels, searching for anyone who might have seen or heard him. There was silence except for the sounds of nature.

The man reached to pull Brody to his feet and then draped him over his shoulders before he headed into the forest. A fifteen minute walk brought him to a cave that he entered. He had already searched for a hiding place for Brody. He just had not expected Brody to walk outside by himself and be distracted by whatever it was that had distracted him. Brody's body was dropped to the cold stone before he was bound and gagged. The man really didn't care if Brody lived or died. If he died, then his father's death would be on Blaze. It was only right. The man walked away, dusting off his hands, heading to find his employer and let him know that the deed had been done.

Looking for his father, Blaze stepped outside and then walked his property around the house and garage. His father's car was still there but there was no sign of his father. Heading back into the house to search, Blaze stopped in the office, reaching for his phone. His father had disappeared and he had no idea where he was.

"Frank? We have a situation. Are you still on duty? You're not? Who is? George? Good. Dad's disappeared. He went outside about an hour ago. I needed to ask him something about one of the charity, a question that has come up. I can't find him anywhere."

Frank drew in a deep breath. This is what they had feared, that Brody or Emily would disappear in an effort to get to Blaze.

"I'm on my way, Blaze. I'll call it in. Stay inside, no matter how much you want to search." Frank merely shook his head at Sue and then ran for his car. This is not how the evening was to go, but it had happened. They now needed to search for Brody. And with Bevin's parents arriving within the hour, that only added to the stress of the situation.

Bevin stared in horror at Blaze as he stood in front of her, a lost look in his eyes and fear on his face.

"What do you mean? Your father's disappeared?" Bevin looked past Blaze at Emily before she was around the man in front of her to hug Emily. "Emily?"

"Blaze is correct. Brody has disappeared. Neither one of us can find him. And Frank and George will be here as well as other officers. I pray that they bring in a K-9 unit as well." Emily walked away to where Mary and Art were waiting, simply waiting to pray with her.

"What can we do, Blaze? We need to be out there searching!" Bevin walked towards the front door, finding Blaze just wrapping his arms around her and stopping her forward walk. "Blaze?"

"We can't go out there right now, sweetheart. It's a crime scene. We need to stay inside." Blaze turned her back towards the office. "Come with me. We'll do some research into what we can. I know the area around here well. This was our retreat on weekends and holidays. I played in these woods. There has to be somewhere that Dad is."

Bevin nodded, looking around the office before she was reaching for a map.

"This map, Blaze? It's a topographical one?"

"It is." Blaze helped to unroll it on the floor, kneeling as he did so. His finger began to trace the area around the cabin, moving further and further away from the cabin as he desperately searched for somewhere his father would be. Brody would not just have walked away from his family, not willingly.

Bevin leaned against Blaze, not realizing that was what she was doing. She was also begging God to lead them to where Brody might be. She bit at her lip for a moment.

"Are there hiding places around here?" Bevin hesitated to ask her question.

Blaze raised his head before he turned to her, a frown in place.

"Hiding places? I'm not sure what you mean."

"You know, hiding places. Like clefts in the rock. Caves. Tunnels." Bevin was grasping at ideas, not sure what to ask. All she could do was ask her questions.

Blaze stared at her for a moment before he was once more staring at the map. A finger tapped on a certain spot before he was on his feet, grabbing Bevin's hand to help her up, and then grasping the map as he almost ran for the door. Flinging it open, Blaze startled the officer standing in front of it, who reached for his gun before he relaxed his hand.

"Blaze?" His question stopped Blaze in his tracks. "What happened?"

"There's a cave about 15 minutes from here." The map shook in Blaze's hand in his agitation. "Here. This spot. Can we check it out?" Blaze's finger stabbed at the map, causing the officer to reach for the paper and take it gently from him.

"We can. Back inside. This would be a prime opportunity for you two to disappear again." The office closed the door after the two before he walked towards Frank.

"Frank? Blaze has a thought. He says there's a cave near here and asked if we could search it."

Frank turned to the officer, reaching for the map even as his eyes searched the house. He saw Blaze and Bevin planted at the living room window watching them.

"We can. And get them away from that window. We have no idea if there are snipers out here or not." Frank walked away, searching for two officers to go with him before he headed in the direction that they would find the cave. He prayed that Blaze was correct and that was where they would find Brody.

Chapter 15

Feeling a hand on her back, Bevin turned almost in fear. The next instant, she was in her mother's arm, hugging her tightly. Her father moved in on her next. They had no idea what they had just walked in on and that worried them.

William and Brenna studied their daughter. They could see the stress in her bearing and wondered at that. They had not seen her for about a year, by her choice, and they just could not understand why.

"Bevin?" William's voice held the question that he would not ask.

"I know, Dad. This is not where you expected to find me. I know. I can't explain it." Bevin was away from them, almost on a run, looking for Blaze.

Blaze watched William and Brenna, not sure what had transpired between Bevin and her parents. He simply wrapped her into another hug and then turned her away from that room. Emily approached the couple, hugging them before she spoke.

"My husband has disappeared in the last hour. We're kind of upset right now." She sniffed back tears.

"Oh, no! And we get dropped into the mix." Brenna didn't know what to say.

"It's okay. We were expecting you. This is not your home town, so we have made arrangements for you to stay here for now. Bevin does need you with her." Emily linked an arm with Brenna, leading her towards the kitchen, William following, feeling lost as he did so.

Art appeared at that moment, stopping William and then leading him away from where the ladies were. He simply pointed to a chair in the sunroom and sat himself before his head was bowed to pray for all involved. That included Bevin's parents.

"What can you tell me about what's going on?" William was direct with his questions.

"Not a lot, I'm afraid. I know that Blaze came to Bevin's rescue and brought her here. They disappeared for a couple of days and then were found. Since then, Bevin has not wanted to leave Blaze's side if she can help it nor does he want to be too far from her." Art shook his head at the question on William's face. "We have no idea what their feelings are for each other. They haven't said."

William nodded. Bevin could and would keep her thoughts to herself. She had always been like that. Nothing that her parents had said to her had ever changed that.

"She's like that. I don't know Blaze so I couldn't speak for him." William was on his feet, intending to find his daughter and speak with her. Only that didn't happen. He watched as Blaze and Bevin disappeared through the front door of the cabin before he had a chance to say anything.

Frank approached the couple, shaking his head. How did they know? They had tracked the cave down and as Blaze had suspected, found Brody there. He was unconscious and on his way even then to the hospital. Frank needed to get Blaze and Emily there but that would be difficult. Bevin would not be left home without Blaze, that much he knew. And with her parents now present, he didn't know how that would work.

"Frank?" Blaze's voice held hope.

"We have your dad, Blaze. He's on his way in. How did you know?" Frank stared at the couple, seeing them exchanging glances.

"God, Frank. It had to be God. Bevin asked if there was anywhere to hide. I had forgotten about that cave. I played in it as a child but haven't been near it since. Dad's okay?"

"He's unconscious at the moment. Where's your mom?" He looked around Blaze as Emily appeared. "Emily? We have Brody. He's on his way in to be examined. Now, the problem will be getting you there."

Emily nodded, knowing that having Bevin's parents there presented a problem but she also knew that Mary and Art would look after them for her.

"Let's go, then." Emily walked towards Frank, her son and his lady following in her footsteps.

Blaze followed his mother towards his father's hospital room, not letting go of Bevin's hand. He just had that horrible sinking feeling that if he did, she would disappear. That he didn't want.

Brody was awake and fighting mad, as he termed it. He had no idea who the man was. Nothing had been said to him but the implied threat towards Blaze was

<hr>

there. He wanted out of the hospital room to investigate that.

"You need to stay for now, Brody." Emily simply stated the facts, finding Brody nodding at last. "You need to do this for us."

"I know. I just want whoever it was." Brody shared a look with Blaze before his gaze stopped on Bevin. "Someone is after our kids, Emily. And I want to know the reason why."

"We all do, Dad, but for now, you need to wait for the IV to finish. Then, we'll head home." Blaze nodded at his father before he headed back out of the room, Bevin keeping step with him. He watched as security guards from their company moved in on his parents and then on them. "It looks as if we have company, sweetheart."

"I know. I don't like it. I want my freedom back." Bevin tugged at her hand, trying to free it from Blaze's grip.

"So do I. And you didn't get a chance to visit with your parents. You should have stayed." Blaze was upset that she had chosen to come with him instead of staying with her parents.

"They will be here for a while. We'll get a chance to visit. It's not like we see each other every day. We're not close, Blaze. We never have been as close as you are with your parents. In fact, I have not physically seen them for a year. We talk about once a week on the phone but we live separate lives." Bevin's voice was so matter of fact that Blaze stopped their walk forward and stared down at her. "It is what it is. I'm not changing just because they're here."

"They will be worried about you, Bevin."

Bevin shrugged, not seeing the compassionate look that Blaze had on his face. She simply found a chair to sit in, watching the people who were seated in the waiting room.

Blaze watched her closely before he sighed. This had to be the relationship that she had with her parents. He was grateful that God had placed him where He did. His parents had supported him all his life in whatever he did, talking through his decisions. Blaze had not been forced to take on the charities. He had chosen to do that, knowing that was where God wanted him.

Chapter 16

Blaze was on his feet early the next morning. He had not slept and needed to. He chose not to, instead spending the night in prayer. Blaze knew that God was the only One who could answer what they were going through. At the moment, that answer was not clear. He reached for paperwork that had appeared on his desk overnight. He was well aware that some of his staff were working on this in conjunction with friends of his. He sighed once more, thinking that seemed to be all he was doing.

Reaching for the coffee carafe, Blaze poured his cup of coffee and then headed for the back deck. It was a favourite spot of his, a place that he called his prayer corner. Today, he needed that solitude to spend even more time with his Heavenly Father. Blaze felt uneasy that morning, certain that something was about to happen and he had no idea what. He needed to find the peace that only God could give.

Bevin too had risen early. She didn't want to face her parents but knew that she had no choice. Blaze and his family had been gracious enough to fly them back to Grasspoint and then offer them a place to stay. She had no answers for them and she knew that they would have multiple questions for her that she was unable or unwilling to answer. She stepped out on to the back desk, pausing as she saw Blaze.

Blaze raised his head as he heard a whisper of sound, his hand reaching for his lady and drawing her down beside him. He wrapped her close to him, sending that she was upset and needed that comfort being close to him would bring. Blaze had finally acknowledged to himself that he loved Bevin and had been searching for her all of his life. He just didn't know her feelings.

"Blaze? Did you learn anything more about what happened last night? Why take your dad and leave him like that?" Bevin was puzzled at that, not realizing that Brody had been taken as a threat levelled towards Blaze.

"He hasn't said anything, not yet. Frank will when he can. I'll speak with him later today. For now, he did say that it was likely a threat towards me. We just don't know why or who."

"And that's the problem, isn't it? Who is doing this and why? Is it because of your work or is it you personally?" Bevin chewed at her lower lip for a moment. "I can see if someone knows of your work and wants to retaliate against you. But your personal life? Who would hate you that much?"

Blaze's hand paused as he was rubbing it on the arm of the glider. He frowned as he looked down at Bevin, finding her staring towards the gardens and trees towards the back of the open area.

"Why would you phrase it like that?" Blaze finally had to just ask.

"I don't know." Bevin shrugged, not even sure that she should have asked that question. "It just seems to personal, what they did. Forcing me onto your property. Kidnapping us. Taking your father and

———

hiding him. They mean you harm, Blaze. Now how do we find out who?"

Blaze grinned down at her as she looked up at him, a frown still on her face.

"We'll work on it, sweetheart. My friends want to help. Do you know Ashlynn and her girls?" When she shook her head, Blaze continued. "I've been friends with Brinn, Chani, Darbi, and Eilis ever since they moved here to live with Ashlynn when their parents died. They went though some rough stuff before they married. We can get together with them if you like and they will work with us to discover who it is. Brinn's father-in-law is a private investigator. He has already likely started an investigation but does not go too far until he has spoken with the victims. Why don't we meet with them this week?"

Bevin sighed. This is not what she wanted, to meet even more people in this town, a town that she fully intended to leave once she knew that Blaze was safe. That was, if her savings held out and she had no idea if they would. This just didn't seem to be going anywhere any too quickly.

"I guess. But Mom and Dad are here. I know I have to spend time with them and I want too\. It's just that Dad will be asking all the questions that he shouldn't. It's what he does." Bevin's head went down on Blaze's shoulder without her realizing that was what she had done.

Blaze didn't move. He liked how Bevin's head felt against him. He had to acknowledge once more that he was in love. He just didn't know if Bevin would love him in return.

"We won't interfere in you meeting with your parents. I got the impression that they wouldn't be staying long. Am I correct?" He watched as Bevin gave a small nod. "Is that how it always is, sweetheart?"

"It is. It's as if they don't need me in their lives despite what they say. I think that is why I ran from home when I could." Bevin was on her feet, moving away from Blaze and the safety that she felt with him. She paused in the doorway to the house to stare back at him, seeing his head bent. The sounds of the early morning critters filled her ears and she smiled for a moment. Bevin decided that she could become accustomed to that and to living here. Only that would never happen. She had fought it out with herself in the early morning hours and had to acknowledge that she loved Blaze. Only, she was certain that he would never return that love.

Mary paused as she was reaching for the ingredients for the breakfast that she was to prepare. Her eyes rested on Bevin for a moment before she was across the room and hugging the younger lady. Mary felt the sobs that Bevin tried hard to control.

"Bevin? What is it?" Mary didn't let the younger lady go.

"It's just everything, I think, Mary. Do you ever come to the point where you are so overwhelmed that you doubt even God cares or hears you?"

"I have been there, Bevin, more times that I can count. God has never left you. He cares so much for you. He wants only His best even though you may face things and events that say otherwise. He has walked this path before you, don't forget that."

Bevin nodded, acknowledging Mary was correct. She walked away from Mary, intent on helping to prepare their meal. She knew that she had to face her parents and dreaded that. Blaze would be gone to his building or be involved in his work in his home office. Bevin felt that she was on her own and didn't like that feeling. She had always been confident in who she was. This adventure or whatever it was called had changed that. And she didn't like it.

Chapter 17

William and Brenna stared at their daughter, shaking their heads in disbelief. There was no way that had happened to her, they decided. It had to be her imagination. But imagination didn't explain what had happened the previous evening.

Bevin had curled up in Blaze's chair near the fireplace in the living room. She had done that deliberately, knowing she needed that contact with him even though he was not there. She faced her parents as they sat across from her.

"That doesn't happen." William was adamant on that. "No one chases you onto someone's business property and threatens you."

"It's the truth, Dad. It really did happen. I lived it." Bevin was on her feet, walking away from her parents.

"Come back here, young lady." William too had risen to his feet, watching as his daughter just kept walking. She had never disobeyed him before and he didn't like it. He had forgotten that she no longer lived under his roof and didn't have to answer to him or obey him. William had always been strict with her and Bevin had been glad in one way to be able to live her own life and make her own decision.

Bevin walked away from her parents, frustrated, stressed, and angry at her father's reaction. It was not what she needed at the time. She needed their support and didn't feel as if she had it. Bevin walked out towards Emily, finding her waiting for her.

"Bevin? What's wrong?" Emily simply hugged her and then turned her to the back door and the swing on the back deck.

"Nothing really. It's what always happens with Dad. He tries to play the heavy-handed father but that never works with me. I just want to run away and hide from him as much as I love him."

"No, you're not the type of person that someone can act like that with. How be we head into town with your mother? We can leave your father with Brody and Art. They'll keep him in line." Emily waited patiently for Bevin to decide, leaving that decision to the younger lady.

"That would work, if we can get Mom away from Dad." Bevin frowned, a thought niggling at the edge of her mind that just didn't come all the way to the forefront.

Emily gave a quick grin and walked back to where Brenna was just standing and staring into space. A quick arm around the other lady had her turning towards where her daughter was waiting. A nod from Brenna had the two ladies quickly gathering their purses and heading for Emily's car. That lady knew at least one security guard would be behind them. It was what their team at the business did. It was not the first time they had had to protect her and not likely would be the last.

Bevin stared around at the people passing by them on the sidewalks. She could feel danger near her and also felt the eyes as everyone else would describe as watching her. She was afraid for both mothers. Emily was taking it all in stride but she could tell that her own mother was upset. Bevin sighed. This was not how the day was to go. All she wanted to do was to go back to Blaze's place and find him, except he was not there.

Blaze turned late that evening as he was walking to his car, security tight to him. His name had echoed across the parking lot. George was walking towards him and Blaze could already tell that he would not like what that man had to say.

George watched Blaze before he was assessing the area around him. Word had reached them not that long ago that an attempt to kidnap the other man even with security around him.

"Blaze? Can we speak for a moment?" George waited as the security with him stopped and then watched around them.

"We can. You're here for a reason." Blaze grew afraid, knowing that the ladies had been out on their own for the day and that he was also being watched very closely. Security had seen evidence of that but had been unable to provide any details. They just weren't there.

"I am. Have you noticed anyone following you today or been around when you've been out and about? And we know that you have been. Our patrols have followed you." George gave a quick grin at Blaze as that man shook his head.

"To tell you the truth? No. When I am with the security team, I concentrate on what I need to concentrate on. They have always made sure that I or Mom and Dad are safe if the need arises. What are you not saying?" Blaze's hand reached to stop George's pacing.

"We received word late this afternoon that you are to disappear again and this time, you won't be coming home. The thinking is that is to find Bevin and draw her out. They can't reach her any other way." George was worried about his friend. He had had a long discussion with Frank who had shaken his head. "We just don't have enough information to know exactly who it is or why or if it does involve Bevin."

Blaze nodded, knowing this was the case. He was not, however, willing to give up his life or his passion for his work. That would never happen, he was adamant on that.

"I see. Mom said that they were followed when they were out today. She also commented that William was growing hostile towards them."

"He is? Any particular reason?" George found that fact interesting even as he watched a car drive slowly by. His hand was on his phone to call in a description and license plate number.

"No, not that she or Dad could tell. Bevin sent me a text after they were home from being out. She doesn't want her parents around her. She feels stifled and put down as she stated, always has with her father. And she doesn't understand why."

———

"Bevin has tasted freedom. You are becoming important to her as well, taking over from William. That could be part of it."

Blaze shook his head.

"I don't think so. She said that he has always been like that to some degree. That's part of the reason that she doesn't see them much." Blaze rubbed at his forehead, a headache beginning. "We need to meet this weekend, George, with Ashlynn and the girls. Bevin needs to hear their stories."

"And we shall. Frank has already reached out to them. Ashlynn is quite willing to host us. She says that you're good friends with her husband now."

Blaze grinned. He was indeed good friends with Torin. They had known each other for years. Torin was a better friend to his father but that was changing. They were being drawn into each other's life just because of Blaze's friendship with the girls.

Chapter 18

Bevin felt the love seat move as someone sat beside her and then an arm around her drew her close to Blaze. She was content to be held by him, she decided, and felt as if she had finally come home. Bevin felt his kiss on her temple and leaned harder against him. She had had words with her father and that meant her parents had packed up and left. In one way, she was sad to see her mother go. In another way, she was content to have them gone. Her father was trying hard to restrict her movements, and she just would not agree with his demands. They were becoming more and more harsh and restrictive.

Brody had stopped Blaze as his son had headed to find Bevin, just letting him know what had happened. Brody was upset at the discord in Blaze's home. Brody and Emily would be moving back home the next day and he was concerned about Blaze and Bevin staying in the same house even with Mary and Art there. Brody was reading William correctly, he decided, and knew that fact would be used against Bevin.

"Okay, sweetheart?" Blaze spoke at last, his voice full of his love for his lady but also concern for her.

Bevin shrugged, snuggling closer to Blaze. She didn't how to word what she needed to say.

"I guess. Dad and I had words."

"Dad said that your parents left. And that your mom wasn't too happy with that."

"She wasn't but she won't go against Dad. She never has." Bevin bit at her lip, praying for the words that she needed to say but not finding them.

"Let me take a guess. He doesn't want you staying here. I can understand to some degree but for now, the police are requesting that we stay together." Blaze stared at the pictures and photos on the opposite wall, particularly the one of a stream running through a forest. "I have a thought. It's not what we need to do. I love you, Bevin, even in such a short time frame that we have known one another. We could marry. That way, he could say nothing about our living under the same roof." Blaze simply waited for Bevin to respond, praying for his lady as he did so.

Bevin sat in shock. Whatever she had expected him to say had not been that. She lifted her face to study him.

"I love you too, Blaze. It's too soon, isn't it?" That question and the adorable look on her face had Blaze bending to kiss her.

"It is soon, but we do love one another, it appears. God has brought us together, I would like to marry you soon. You need to hear the stories of some friends of mine. Ashlynn and her nieces went through some rough stuff but are all happily married. Frank has asked if we could all meet on Saturday as a group. I think that we need to but that decision is yours to make." Once more, Blaze waited for Bevin to speak.

Bevin was in shock. There was no way that his friends would want to meet with her. On the other hand, if someone had gone through anything remotely like what they were now involved in, she wanted to hear about it.

"I think that's a good idea. Where?"

"At Torin and Ashlynn's. They have a really nice place. And it has security. He's a multi-millionaire and has had threats over the years. Casual is fine. In fact, you would not know Torin is rich. He doesn't flaunt his wealth." Blaze grew silent, simply content to sit and hold the lady he loved.

Bevin walked the house the next morning, in a daze. Blaze had found her, kissed her, told her that he loved her, and then slipped a beautiful ruby ring on her finger. She had watched him leave for his office reluctantly before she turned. Emily was waiting for her, to hug her and welcome her to their family. Bevin knew the reaction that she would get from her father. She just didn't know the reaction her mother would have.

"Bevin? Have you too made any plans as yet?" Emily waited for Bevin to respond. The ladies had taken over Blaze's home office for the morning.

"Not yet. It's all too new. I want this, whatever it is, over. I fear for him." Bevin was sober as she spoke. She had spoken with Frank earlier and he had simply said that they had no idea who it was or why. There just wasn't enough information to determine that.

—

"We all do. Now, let's find some paper and pen. I sent one of our guys to find your mom and bring her here. I talked with her earlier. She is adamant that she is not being left out of such an important day for you as this." Emily hugged Bevin again as she saw the tears the younger lady was trying to hard to hide.

"Thank you, Emily. I do want Mom here. It's Dad that's the issue." Bevin found her favourite chair in Blaze's office.

"Why is that, Bevin? Has he always been to like that? If he has, I don't blame you for running away from home." Emily grinned at her as Mary approached. "Mary, you need to join us. We are planning Bevin and Blaze's wedding once Brenna arrives."

Mary reached to hug Bevin, holding on as she felt the sobs that Bevin would not shed.

"I think this is wonderful. And yes, I will join you. I just need to find our teas, coffees, and sweets." Mary was away and back with a tray that she set on the coffee table in front of the couch, Brenna following her.

Brenna hugged her daughter, sorrowing that William's attitude and desire to control his only child had reached this point. They had had words the night before, something that they had never done before. Brenna had simply taken her luggage and moved to a different motel, one where he could not find her easily. Blaze had helped her to do that, having a long conversation with her over the phone as he did. Brenna

—

98

had been grateful for his assistance, knowing that would not sit well with William.

"Where do we start, Bevin?" Brenna had her pad of paper and pen ready to write.

"With prayer, Mom. We can't go on without that. And we do need to solve this, whatever it is, we're just not getting too far." Bevin sighed. "We're meeting with Blaze's friends tomorrow for a meal. He assures me that they will have been working on it even without our input."

Chapter 19

Running for a nearby store later that morning, Blaze could hear the pounding footsteps that seemed to be growing closer with each step that his feet hit the pavement. He swerved around the pedestrians, finding the doorway that he wanted and shoving through the door. He snapped the lock on even as his friend watched in shock.

"To the back, Blaze. You know where to hide." Jake watched as Blaze disappeared before he was at the door, the blinds pulled down and the sign flipped to read that the store was closed. He could hear the pounding at the door and backed away, heading for where Blaze had hidden.

"Jake?" Blaze kept his voice low, peeking out of a doorway.

"They are really trying to get in. And I'm not about to let them. What is going on?" Jake spun to stare at his lifelong friend.

"I'm in the middle of something, Jake. You know? One of those adventures that our friends have had?" Blaze grinned for a moment before he sobered. "And I do need to look at rings."

Jake stared once more and then harder at his friend before he sighed.

"What did you go and do, Blaze?"

"I came to the aid of a beautiful lady and fell in love. She loves me as well. We're planning on getting married soon." Blaze's face lit up as he spoke about his lady love.

"She's the one that you rescued from your property?" At Blaze's nod, Jake headed back into the store, checking to see that the men had indeed left. "They're gone for now, Blaze. We'll need some of your security people to get you out of here. And you were walking on your own, weren't you?"

Blaze sighed. He had been and that likely had not been a good idea, not at this time. He just refused to let anyone dictate how he lived. Only that had to change now that Bevin would be in his life.

"Not likely a good idea, I suspect, Jake. Now, what can you show me in ruby or emerald rings? Rose gold, I think." Studying the rings shown to him, he made his selection with the understanding that he could return and exchange them.

Jake's hand stopped him from moving to the door.

"Call your office and have someone meet you at the back door. But first, Blaze, let me pray with you. You're in danger, your lady is in danger, and I hear that your father had been harmed. You need God's protection right now. It's not easy to begin a married life in normal situations. This is far from normal."

"It is. I know what Ashlynn and her girls went through. I was praying that my friends avoided it. I just didn't pray that I would. I should have."

"You should have and your parents likely were praying that way. That's not how God works. He allows sunshine and rain in our lives. Just because we're His doesn't mean that we won't face anything. He walks before us and beside us. Just remember that you were prayed for in the garden all those years ago. Keep your hand in God's and follow His leading and nudges."

"I know, Jake. It's hard though when someone you love is threatened and you have no idea why or from whom. I want to take her out as we should be able to do, but having security with us all the time sort of quenches the romance." Blaze grinned at Jake's laugh. "It does."

"I know that it can but you will get through this. You might not like what you or Bevin, is it, has to face. That's life, unfortunately. We are called to be those witnesses for him in any circumstance. This is no different." Jake turned as he heard a tap at the back door. "Stay here, Blaze."

Blaze had his phone out.

"It's Jasper. He's at the back door, waiting for me." Blaze began to laugh. "He has three cars with him, just to confuse whoever it might be who is watching."

"And all your cars look similar." Jake began to laugh as well. "Let's get you out of here and to where you need to be."

Blaze stared down at the paperwork that had appeared on his desk. His secretary stood in front of the desk, a puzzled look on her face.

"I didn't put that there." Cara was adamant on that. "I have not seen it before."

"I didn't think that you had. Let me check with security." He looked around as Jasper appeared. "Jasper?"

"Blaze? We had a break in security while you were out." He pointed towards Blaze's desk. "And that seems to be why."

"Call Frank or whoever it is that you need to. I'll move to another office for now. Cara? You're okay?"

"I am, Blaze. Just angry that someone managed to get in. I didn't see anyone. The only time that I was gone was for my breaks and lunch other than when I had to do some photocopying. That only took five minutes." Cara was frustrated as well that someone had managed to get into the building and to Blaze's office.

Blaze nodded. He knew that Cara was very conscientious about staying at her desk.

"It's okay, Cara. We'll need to move away from the office for now." He sighed, not wanting to know who it was. It had to be someone he knew that had done this. "Once you've given your statement, take off for the day. And take Monday as well. I intend to. You need a long weekend."

Cara reached to hug her boss before she turned to gather what she could before she stopped. That wouldn't be allowed, she knew.

"We can't take anything from here, now can we?" She walked away, leaving Blaze staring after her before he shared a look with Jasper.

"She's right, Blaze. Everything has to stay here for now." Jasper planted himself outside of the office door, on guard for the boss whom everyone liked and would do just about anything for.

Chapter 20

Bevin paced the cabin, not seeing the comfortable colours and furnishings. She was troubled and kept staring at the piece of paper in her hand. She was alone in the cabin for the moment, the others having to be away. That didn't frighten her. What frightened her was the names that she had come up with. She didn't like some of them. Bevin considered them friends but she now wondered just how much of a friend that they were to her.

Blaze dropped his briefcase in his office before he headed to change to more casual clothes. He returned to the living room and simply stopped to watch his lady as she paced. He moved in on her and wrapped her in a hug.

Bevin jumped as she felt arms around her and then was hugging Blaze. He was safe and she could relax. Or could she?

'Have a good day, sweetheart?" Blaze waited patiently for Bevin to respond.

"I did, I think. We have to go over our wedding plans. My mom, your mom, and Mary helped sort everything out. We're not having a big one, are we?" Bevin stared up at the handsome man staring down at her.

"No, we're not. Neither one of us wants that. Listen. We need to talk but first, I have something for you." Blaze drew her to a seat on the couch in the living room, pulling out a bag. He opened a small box to retrieve the emerald ring that he had chosen. "I love you so much, Bevin, more each day. Will you accept this as a token of my love?" He waited patiently for her to study his face and then his hand holding the ring before she studied the ring, nodding at last. He slipped it on her finger and then kissed her. "Thank you for trusting me."

"We have come to know each other better than we would have if we had just started dating." Bevin cuddled closer to Blaze, suddenly deeply afraid for her knight. "I've come up with a list of names that I need to go over with Frank."

"You have." Blaze didn't comment any further. Frank would be around that evening, he had simply stated. The pair of them needed to stay out of danger. Could they do that? "Frank is dropping out this evening. I need to tell you what happened today." Blaze did just that, drawing a shocked exclamation from Bevin.

"To get into your office like that? It has to be someone you know."

"Maybe. Frank has the security feed and has the crime lab going over it. And no, they are not making us a priority. He decides what is important, not us." Blaze settled back, tucking Bevin closer to him. "Those plans? Care to share"

Bevin nodded before she looked up at him.

"We need to pray, Blaze. I fear for us and for our families. Dad and Mom had words last night, she said, and said that you helped her move to another motel."

———

"I did, and it was at her request. She needed a break from your father. How much does he control her?" Blaze had hesitated to ask that question.

Bevin nodded, knowing that Blaze had gone to the very centre of her parents' relationship.

"A lot, I think. Mom has never complained but there are times when I see that she is frustrated and wanting to leave. That doesn't happen in our families. No matter how abusive a relationship is, the couple stays together. I don't know what will happen with them. Mom is adamant that she is not going back if things stay the same."

"And that's why you ran, isn't it?" Blaze studied the dark oak flooring under his feet, what he could see of it. He was frustrated that this was happening to his lady and his lady's mother. How it played into what they were going through was not clear. He was convinced that it did somehow. Blaze had reached out to Emma the night before, just asking her to investigate Bevin's father. He had still to hear back from her.

"Blaze? Where do we go from here?" Bevin knew that she loved the tall handsome man holding her and that he loved her in return. "How much danger are we in if we continue with our plans?"

Blaze shrugged, having had that conversation with Frank earlier that day. Frank had been open with Blaze, the uncertainty of what the couple was facing weighing heavily on them all.

"I talked to Frank earlier today and asked him that. He wasn't sure how it played into it. He would be researching it as well." Blaze's eyes closed for a moment as fatigue hit and then he prayed for his lady and her mother once more.

"And you have reached out to Emma?" Bevin felt his nod. Of course, he would. It was what he did. He was trying to take care of her and protect her. "When will we hear?"

"I don't know, sweetheart. At some point, we will. For now, what plans have you come up with?" Blaze grinned as she shook a finger at him.

"Plans? Our wedding plans?" Bevin leaned towards the end of the couch, reaching across Blaze to retrieve a folder. "This is what we decided. We are keeping it very small. Just family and close friends." Bevin bit at her lip. "I don't know now about Dad being there. And I don't have close friends. I've moved too much in the last few years to have that."

Blaze simply hugged her tighter, a prayer whispering in her ear, a prayer for peace and safety.

"It's okay, sweetheart. I don't have many. I know Ashlynn's girls will move in and become just that for you. We're meeting with them tomorrow at Torin and Ashlynn's place. Are you still okay with that?" Blaze waited patiently for Bevin to think through that and whether they would be safe.

"We won't bring them any more danger, will we?" Bevin's elbow dug into Blaze's ribs as he snickered for a moment. "This is not funny, buster." An answering grin was on her face.

"I know it's not but we'll be okay there. It's getting there and back that we have to worry about.

And our company security will look after that." Blaze sighed. "This is not how we're supposed to be doing this. We should be free to come and go, just as in the past."

"And until we find out whoever it is and they are arrested, we can't. Just how much danger are we bringing to the community at large?" Bevin didn't expect Blaze to answer. There was just no answer for that. Her eyes closed as her head went down on his shoulder and she slept. Her sleep had been troubled for years. With Blaze in her life and making her feel safe, cherished, and loved, her lack of sleep was catching up with her.

Blaze tilted his head to study his lady, looking up as Mary approached.

"It's okay, Blaze. She said that she's not been sleeping." Mary set down the tray with their mugs of coffee on it beside him on the little table. "I'll be back with fresh coffee for her when she wakes up. You make her feel safe and cherished, you know. You have waited years for God to lead you to your lady. Bevin's that lady." Mary reached to give him a hug and then walked away, her own prayers raising for the young man whom she had seen grow from a baby to the man he was now.

Chapter 21

The next afternoon, Bevin's footsteps slowed as she stared at the house in front of her. It was like Blaze's, she decided, just an ordinary house holding extraordinary secrets. Her hand tightened on Blaze's as he waited patiently for her to continue forward.

"This is his home?" Bevin could not stop herself from asking.

"It is. He doesn't flaunt his wealth. Instead, he uses it for God." Blaze tugged her forward as he saw Torin waiting for them. "Torin? Good to see you again. This is Bevin, my intended." Blaze grinned as Bevin gave him a bit of attitude.

"Blaze. So good to see you are okay." Torin reached to shake his friend's hand and then simply hugged Bevin. "Sorry, Bevin, we're huggers. I hope that you don't mind."

Bevin stared at him for a moment, not sure how to respond.

"And if I did?" Bevin was challenging Torin and the three of them knew that.

"Then we would share your hand instead. Come on in. We're in the office for now." Torin walked back into his home.

Blaze turned in a circle, feeling watched. He knew that would happen. He had prayed for that not to happen that day but it had.

Late that afternoon or was it early evening, Bevin wasn't sure, Blaze tucked her into his vehicle before he slid behind the wheel. He reached to kiss his lady before he just sat, making no move to drive away. He couldn't. He could sense someone wanting for them.

"Blaze?" Bevin's voice held the question that she wouldn't ask.

"Someone is out there. The security team is almost here. We'll wait for them." His head turned her way. "Have a good time today, sweetheart?"

"I did. I wasn't sure what to expect. They are a wonderful group. They just opened up and let me in."

Blaze grinned. He had known that was what they would do. He just hadn't been sure if Bevin would accept this. Apparently, she had. The men had heard the ladies' laughter over the afternoon as they met separately and then together.

"It's what they do, sweetheart." Blaze was growing more anxious. The security team had not appeared and he had had no word from them. He should have had. "I don't like this, Bevin. The team should be here by now." His phone was out as he called the security team. "For some reason, they can't get down the road." Blaze looked around before he drove away from the front entrance. "There is another road in that is not known to anyone. Torin showed it to me one day. We'll leave that way."

Bevin was suddenly deeply afraid, if not terrified. She had not expected their afternoon to end this way, with them on the run from the bad guys as Brinn called them. She had come to appreciate the five ladies over the afternoon, being accepted into their group.

"Blaze? Can we get away?" Bevin's hand tightened on her seat belt.

"Pray that we do. I'm praying that Torin is correct and we can get away." His phone was tossed towards her. "Send a message to Gerry and let him know where we are. He can meet up with us there."

Blaze hesitated as he reached the road, not seeing anyone who should be there. He gunned the motor and took off in a direction away from town, desperate to find somewhere they could be safe. He just didn't know it it would work.

Gerry slowed his vehicle as he approached the lane to Torin's home, seeing the tire tracks leading away from it. His phone was out as he called Blaze, not receiving any answer. This is not how he wanted it. His next call was to the police, asking for assistance.

Frank walked towards Gerry as he stood outside of his car, leaning against it as it sat in front of Blaze's lane.

"Where is he?" Frank's voice was harsh with worry.

"Not where he's supposed to be. He let me know where to find him but he wasn't there. We're looking, Frank, but not having any success in finding him." Gerry was both worried and frustrated.

"None of our patrols have either. He's gone into hiding somewhere or else he's been stopped and disappeared again." This was not what anyone wanted but it was a distinct possibility. Frank listened to the night sounds of nature and then squinted at the cloud over that hid the moon and stars. "We're not going to be able to search tonight. Head off, Gerry. We'll meet again in the morning."

Frank walked back along the road outside of Torin's property. He sighed. There were more tire tracks that he expected. That meant that someone knew about the hidden lane and had followed Blaze as he had sped away to what he prayed had been safety. Frank was back in his car, slowly following the tracks. His foot hit the brake suddenly and he was out of his car, heading for the side of the road. A glint of metal had shown in his headlights. A hand was on his weapon as he approached the vehicle, realizing that it did indeed belong to Blaze.

A whisper of sound caught his attention. In the time it took for him to register that someone was there, Frank went down under a harsh blow from a piece of wood. He lay sprawled on the crushed grass from the SUV, not hearing the evil laugh from his assailant.

Alarm was raised early the next morning when it became evident that Frank was not responding to any calls. Patrol officers scattered to search for their fellow officer.

George headed for the hidden entrance and then the road leading away from it. An exclamation was torn from his body as he found Frank's car and radioed for help. His car door slammed behind him as he frantically began to search, finding the dew had removed any trace of Frank's footsteps. He headed towards the trees on the side of the road, hesitating for a moment before he broke into a run, dropping to his knees beside his fellow detective. Frank was alive but unconscious. The area soon was swarming with officers and paramedics.

George walked towards the truck, his gloved hand reaching for the door handle. It was as he suspected. Blaze and Bevin were missing. It was as if they didn't exist. There was no evidence that could be found to show what had happened to them.

Walking through the hospital corridors, George was lost in thought. They had no idea where the couple was or even if they were still alive. They had a senior detective down and unconscious, having lain in the elements all night. The officers were scrambling to decipher what had happened but there were few clues. Frank needed to be awake to speak with them. They had no idea when that would happen. Sue was at his side, refusing to leave even when asked. An officer stood at the hospital room door and nodded at George as he hesitated to enter.

Chapter 22

A day later, Frank was on his feet and back at his desk despite his physician's orders. Sue had asked that he not go in but she knew that he would. All she could do was pray for him and pray for their friends who were still missing.

Frank pulled back his desk chair, still shaky on his feet. He knew that he needed to be at home on sick leave but he refused. He also needed to find Blaze and Bevin. To have them disappear once more was not what anyone of them wanted. Frank knew the area where they had disappeared. He had been part of a search for a small child in that area just in the last six months. Thankfully, that child was found alive. He didn't know if Blaze and Bevin would be.

George hesitated a moment before he approached Frank's office and then sat in front of the older man's desk. He didn't speak, spending the time waiting in prayer.

"Frank? Should you even be here?" George finally had to ask. He knew the answer but he also knew Frank.

"No, I shouldn't but I have to be. I need to do this." Frank slumped back in his chair, exhaustion already wiping out his strength.

"No, you need to be at home." George was around the desk, hauling Frank to his feet, and then locking Frank's door after them. "Go home, Frank. I'll work this as I can. You need to take care of yourself. Blaze would want that." He watched as Frank nodded and then walked away. George knew that Sue was waiting for Frank. She had never gone home after dropping her husband at the detachment.

Settled down in his office at home, Frank looked around. Sue stood nearby, watching him carefully before she walked away to answer the door. Richard and Don stood there as did Abe and Emma. She shrugged and pointed towards the office. The three men walked that way before Emma's arm was around her and drawing her into the welcoming kitchen, decorated in whites and yellows.

"Sue? What do you know about what happened?" Emma watched the older lady carefully. It was not the first time that she had asked that question of the lady.

"What do I know? Other than that Blaze and Bevin have disappeared. I spoke with her mom. She's on her way here. I don't know where her father is. There seems to be a break in that marriage and I don't understand why." Sue was sober as she spoke, knowing that if she needed information on that, she would be told.

"Yes, that's what I've been told." Emma didn't state but it was Brenna what had reached out to her, just asking for her to look into her husband. She was ready to leave him but she wanted proof of what he had done. Neither lady had expressed their thoughts, that just maybe William was involved in all of this.

"I fear for Bevin and Blaze. They had plans made to marry and were looking at doing that in the next two weeks. Now, I'm not sure that those plans will ever come to life." Sue blinked back tears as she spoke, her hands busy all the while in making coffee and finding something to eat to go with it. She knew that time was important to find them. She didn't think, however, that they would find them in time.

Brenna watched the men work away before she sighed. William should be here but she had not spoken to him in a couple of days. That should have worried her, but it didn't. All she could think of was her daughter and her knight and pray that they came home safely. There was no guarantee on that, not from how she was reading the men. The two ladies approached her and drew her away, just to spend time in prayer with her. Brenna was grateful for that, not having had that in a few years. William had been more controlling on where she spent her time and seemed to resent her attendance at any meeting at the church that he could not be with her at.

Frank looked around late that afternoon. He was on his feet, heading for the back door, hearing a sound there. Sue had had to leave for a meeting, not that she wanted to but she needed to be there. He stood for a moment, staring at the door, rubbing at the sore spot on the back of his head. His headache had increased over the day and he had finally had to admit to it and take medication to try and quell the pain. It wasn't working out so well.

His hand on the lock, Frank cautiously opened the door. He frowned at Will and Bob, two undercover officers, who stood there, Will with his back to the door as he surveilled the area.

———

"What are you two doing here?" Frank's voice was rough from the pain that he was in. "Get in here." He shut and locked the door behind them. They would not be there unless there was a reason for them to be there.

"Blaze is missing?" Bob spoke for the duo. They had been involved in bringing others who had been kidnapped home and in general, helping to drive down crime in their city.

"He is. So is Bevin. What do you two know about that?" Frank reached out a shaking hand to find a chair, sitting on it before he embarrassed himself and ended up face down on the floor.

Bob nodded even as he worked to prepare something for them to eat. It was not the first time that they had done that.

"That's what we heard. Rumours are rife on the street about it, but we can't confirm anything as yet. What are your thoughts?" Will sat across the table from Frank, a frown on his face. "And just how are you? Don't tell us that you are fine. We know better."

"No, I'm not fine. I didn't see whoever it was and I want them. I had just found the truck and was walking towards it when I was taken down." Frank was angry at that, knowing that he had to let God have his anger. "I worry about Blaze and Bevin. They have a lot going on that we can't track down."

"We know that they do." Bob finally sat, a thumb rubbing at the mug of coffee that sat in front of him. "What can we do for them?"

"Find them. We need to do that and soon. I fear for their lives. We haven't got a good handle of what is going on with them or why or who. What do you two know?"

Will and Bob exchanged a glance. They didn't know much more than the couple were in danger and then had disappeared. The people on the street were helping to search. Blaze had taken care of many of them over the months and years. He didn't hesitate to reach out to the resources that were needed for them. The street people desperately wanted to pay him back in some way.

Chapter 23

A day later, Will tracked Frank down on a crime scene, making sure that Frank knew that he was there and then stepped back into the shadows of a building to wait for that investigator to finish and then find him. Frank had nodded at Will before his attention went back to the murder scene that he was on. It made no sense, he decided, that the older man had been killed. He was known in his neighbourhood to be generous and caring and willing to help anyone out. It would take a long time, Frank decided, to reach the conclusion as to who had killed him.

Tucking away his notepad and pen at last, Frank sighed. He was exhausted and still in pain from a headache. He didn't like feeling that way. Ashlynn had reached out to him the night before, worried about her friend. He had laughed at her and told her that he was coping. But what all had she really wanted to ask him? Her keen questions about Blaze and Bevin had stopped his words before he was nodding. Ashlynn just might be on to something. He was well aware that Garrett, one of her nieces' father-in-law, was investigating what was happening to their friend and that he would have reached out to others.

Walking towards Will, Frank simply followed that man to a diner and slid into a booth. His eyes closed for a moment as he sat, grateful for that. They opened to find Will staring at him, a worried look on his face.

"What do you have, Will?" Frank kept his voice low, knowing that Will and Bob would have found something for one of them to seek him out.

"We know where they are. Bob's watching the building." Will kept his head down, trying to act as someone down and out on their luck.

Frank paused before he nodded. His eyes were searching the customers in the diner, not feeling as if he was being watched.

"Where?"

"Just outside of town, near Blaze's other cabin. There's a rundown shack that they are in. I don't know if we even knew that it was there. We haven't been able to get in to try and free them." Will knew that he and Bob would try again that night. Time seemed to be of the essence from what they were told. Someone on the inside had reached out to them and provided the location. "We're moving in tonight. Once we have them, we'll give you the location. For now, we need to keep it quiet. If it's found out, they will likely moved and then we're starting all over." Will was on his feet, moving away before Frank could ask any further questions.

Frustrated at the turn of events, Frank sipped at his coffee before he dropped money on the table to pay for the coffees and walked away. He was needed back in the office for an interview, an interview that he had no desire to do. He sighed. Things were heating up for his friends, and he just didn't know if he had it in him any more to continue as an investigator. That was something that he and Sue were praying through.

———

Under cover of the cloud-covered night sky, Will and Bob crept closer to the shack, their heads turning as they watched for anyone approaching them. It was quiet, except for the night sounds. That was a relief in one way. In another, it was concerning that the couple were likely on their own.

Bob's hand reached for a loose board at the back of the shank, listening carefully for any sound from within in. There was none. That concerned them as they would have thought to hear something. Stepping in quickly, Bob's small flashlight glimmered briefly, shining in eyes that were watching them. Will was beside him, moving towards the dark forms that they could see.

"Blaze?" Bob kept his voice barely audible. "Are you able to walk?"

"Untie me and we'll see. We've been kept tied up most of the time." Blaze surged to his feet, finding the pins and needles sensation that he expected to feel not as bad as he thought. "Let's get out of here." His hand reached for Bevin's, not finding it. "Where's Bevin?"

"Will's already got her out. Now, move." Bob was certain that he could hear noise heading their way. He didn't want to be caught there or out in the open.

Blaze moved as quickly as he could, heading away from the shack and in the direction that Bob had pointed him to. He had no idea how they had been found. He was just glad that they had been and that they were free. Catching up with Will and Bevin, Blaze paused, turning to look behind him.

"Where are the men?" Bevin's voice, though low, did sound loud in the sudden quiet. Her hand clapped across her mouth in sudden fear.

"They are not around, Bevin." Will walked away from the others, searching for a moment before he was back and motioning them forward. "We need to get you two out of here and now."

Bob shoved at Blaze, who turned with a stern look on his face. Bob sighed. Blaze just wasn't moving as quickly as he should. Part of that was the maltreatment that he seemed to have suffered at the hands of their abductors.

"I'm moving." Blaze was becoming combative, not his usual self. "Where to?"

"Straight ahead of you, Blaze." Bob watched with slight amusement as Bevin reached for Blaze's hand and pulled him with her. "That's right, Blaze. Bevin has the right idea." He watched as the other three moved quietly and quickly away from him before he turned and studied what he could see of the shack. He then ran after them, eyes alert and searching around them. They seemed to have just been able to walk away from the shack. That just didn't happen. God had intervened once more in a rescue.

Turning in surprise as they were not taken to Blaze's home, Bevin's mouth opened to ask a question before she snapped it closed. She had no idea who these two men were but Blaze seemed to know them and trust them. Bevin had to rely on Blaze's connection with them and she wasn't sure that she could. She looked around the rundown exterior of the building on the outskirts of town, somewhat reluctant to move into it. Blaze's hand was tight on hers as he pulled her forward.

"It's okay, Bevin. It's okay. We'll be safe here, or at least as safe as we can be anywhere right now. Will and Bob are actually officers. I suspect that they have already sent in other officers to the shack." Blaze wrapped Bevin tightly into his arms, knowing that she was scared and uncertain of herself and the two men. He had to admit that he was scared as well. This, whatever this was, was trying his trust in his fellow men. Blaze looked up at the ceiling of the room that they were in, a mouthed thank you to God. He had protected them from death although that had been threatened and provided a way out of their predicament.

"Are you sure?" Bevin shoved away from Blaze, pacing the room, not seeing Will as he stepped back inside.

Blaze and Will shared a look. Will nodded at the question of Blaze's face. Their abductors were arrested, having returned to the shack and walking into the arms of law enforcement. The couple just needed to stay where they were for now.

Looking around as more footsteps approached the door, Will stepped back outside. Frank was there, looking rather rough for wear as the saying went. He nodded, speaking quietly with him before Frank was past him and in the room. He stared at the couple who were staring back at him.

"You're safe." Frank nodded at Blaze. "We'll talk, Blaze, Bevin. For now, we need to have you assessed by a physician. Come on, then." He waited patiently for Bevin to make a move, which she didn't seem inclined to do. He studied the room that they were in. It was nothing like the rundown condition of the building. Will and Bob had worked to make it safe and at least presentable over the months that they had been undercover. It was their safe haven. Frank wondered how safe it would be now that they had used it for Blaze and Bevin.

Blaze's head dropped for a moment as he waited somewhat impatiently for Bevin to make a move. She didn't seem inclined to do that. He reached for her hand, tugging her with him towards the door and then to Frank's car. Neither one saw the officers that surrounded them. Their whole focus was the short walk from the building to the vehicle.

Frank sped away from the downtown area, other patrol vehicles escorting them, heading for the hospital. The couple needed to be assessed, he knew, just to ensure that there were no injuries. They didn't seem to be injured but there was always that possibility. Besides, he needed that assessment as part of the investigative process.

"Blaze? Bevin? Are either one of you injured?" Frank shot a look at the pair in the backseat of his car. He gave a grim smile. They just were not letting go of one another.

"No, I don't know that we are. They roughed Blaze up some but not what I was expecting." Bevin studied Blaze. "We were tied up most of the time. The men only came around twice a day to bring us food and water."

Blaze was nodding, his eyes on his beloved Bevin.

"It was strange, Frank. They came in, took us away, and then just tied us up in that shack. It's as if they were waiting for orders on what to do with us that never came." Blaze was puzzled by that.

Assessed and then released, the couple found themselves once more in Frank's car. Blaze studied his friend, seeing the way that Frank was moving and knowing that he shouldn't be on duty. He sighed to himself. Frank would do that, just because they were friends and also because that was his character.

"Are our parents okay?" Blaze finally had to ask.

"Your parents are, Blaze. Your mom is, Bevin. The thing is that your father has disappeared. We can't find him anywhere despite searching for him. Any idea where he might have gone?" Frank watched Bevin for a moment in the rearview mirror.

Bevin shrugged. She had no idea where her father would be. She suspected that he had been behind this abduction or whatever it was, but she had no proof. Bevin was scared, she had to admit, more scared than she had ever been. Her hand found Blaze's, her grip tight on his.

"I don't know, Frank. I wonder if he was the one behind this, in order to prevent us from getting married." Bevin looked up at Blaze, finding him watching her closely. "Blaze?"

"I wondered that as well, sweetheart. I truly did. It felt more like an amateur than someone who had done this before. I don't want to accuse your father without proof." Blaze's eyes turned to the outside of the car, studying his home. He was glad to be home. He just didn't know how long that would last before they disappeared once more.

"We'll do our best to find him." Frank opened his door, not feeling any danger at present. "Let's get you two inside. We have people waiting for you." He walked behind them as they almost ran for the front door, a hand on his service revolver. He was taking no chances on them disappearing again before they were safely inside.

Brody and Emily turned as they heard the front door open and then close before footsteps headed for the kitchen. Emily was in the hallway, her hands covering her mouth before she was reaching to hug Blaze and then Bevin.

"Where were you two? And how did you get home?" Brody hugged his son and then Bevin, standing with an arm around Bevin's shoulders.

"Frank brought us. We'll talk, Dad, but first we need to clean up." Blaze reached for Bevin's hand, walking away from his parents. Neither one heard a soft sound as Brenna appeared behind his parents.

"They're home?" Brenna was in shock before she turned to Frank, a frown on her face.

Frank grinned at her even as he moved towards the kitchen. He studied the room, seeing how Blaze had designed it to keep in character with the cabin but so that it had the modern conveniences that he wanted. Mary had worked with him on that, Frank knew.

"They're okay?" Brody moved towards Frank, a question on his face.

"They are, physically, for the most part. I'll find someone for them to speak with." Frank had done that in the past with victims of crime. "They are victims, Brody, whether or not that they will admit it."

"They are. Blaze has a charity that he works with for those particular people. I never thought that he would ever need it himself." Brody frowned as Frank's hand went up. "Frank?"

"We need to find someone outside of his organization for him to speak with. He can't speak with his own people." Frank reached into his shirt pocket, withdrawing a folded piece of paper. "I would suggest that he contact this lady. She's been through a lot herself besides being a retired forensics psychologist. Darci has called me, providing a profile of who is behind it. She is always accurate with those profiles."

Blaze had appeared at that point, reaching to take the piece of paper from Frank. Unknown to either man with him, Blaze had reached out to Darci in the past for aid with those who needed it. She would be in touch, he knew.

"I'll call her, Frank. Now, Dad, what do we do next?" He turned to his father, the look of a little boy on his face who didn't know what to do next.

It almost broke Brody's heart to see that vulnerable look on his son's face, one that he had not seen in far too many years. Whatever had been done or said to his son had caused him to doubt his ability to function and move forward. Brody had no doubt that Bevin had been threatened to cause this depth of despair in Blaze.

———

Chapter 25

Bevin faced off against Blaze, standing on the opposite side of the couch from him. Her arms were wrapped around herself as she fought to keep the smile from her face. Her boyfriend as everyone was calling him wanted her to go out for a meal. Bevin wanted that too. She was just uncertain as to how safe they would be. She had had a long talk with Frank. Frank had been honest with her. They had to set aside the investigation. There just wasn't enough information for them to continue it at the present time despite the abduction.

"We can't stop living our lives, sweetheart. Besides, we need to come up with a wedding date. We can discuss that." Blaze had an irresistible look on his face before he simply walked around the couch and hugged his lady.

"I know, Blaze. We have to continue to live. But how do we do it? We can't have security following us everywhere. They have lives too."

"I know that they do." Blaze groaned as his phone chimed with a text message. It had been doing that constantly all day he thought. He was ready to drop his phone on the desk in his home office and walk away from it for a while.

"You need to see who that it." Bevin tilted the hand that he held the phone in. "Who's that?"

"Abe? He has a security team that we may need to call in. He also has two other friends, Richard and

Don, with security teams. More importantly, Abe's wife, Emma, has a business to find people, places, and whatnot that no one else can. Tomorrow's Sunday. They want to meet with us. That means that Emma has found information for us and likely already forwarded it on to Frank." Blaze looked down as Bevin sighed, moving closer to him.

"About Frank? He looks rough. He should have taken time off." Bevin was worried about him, worried that he would be hurt even worse or burn out under the investigations that he had underway.

"He'll adjust, sweetheart. It's what he does. They'll make sure that he takes time off. It's what they do." Blaze turned her towards the door. "For now, we're not hiding any more. If it's okay with you, let's go out for a meal."

Bevin sighed to herself. Blaze was trying hard, almost too hard, to ensure that she was safe and unharmed. But it wasn't up to him. It was up to God.

"Where is God in all this, Blaze?" Bevin asked the question that all the couples who had had adventures over time had asked.

"He's right here, sweetheart. Right here with us. He never leaves us. He is protecting us although it doesn't seem like it. He doesn't allow anything to happen to us that is not in His will for us. He will hide us and cover us in the cleft of the rock when needed. He has walked this path before us. We were prayed for in the garden all those years ago." Blaze stopped, knowing that he could continue but that Bevin already knew the answers to what he was saying.

Bevin listened carefully as Blaze spoke, knowing that he was correct. She just felt at the moment that God was not there with her. Bevin knew better as Blaze had correctly stated.

"Okay, then, where for a meal? I'm not dressing up." Bevin scowled at Blaze as he grinned at her and then hugged her once more.

"We can pick something up and eat at the park by the lake. It is usually busy at this time of day. We should be safe in a crowd. Or not." Blaze studied the lady in front of him. "I know what you're thinking, that we are putting others at risk. We are. Every couple whom I have spoken with who had adventures such as this have said the same."

Bevin shoved away from Blaze, pacing the living room. She caught a glimpse of Mary and Art as they passed by towards the kitchen.

"You keep talking about all these couples. I don't know them. And I should if they're friends, shouldn't I?"

Blaze nodded. Bevin had asked the question that he had been asking himself, how to reach out to his friends without overwhelming his lady.

"We can do that. Abe's security team all went through stuff. How be we ask some of them to come with Abe and Emma tomorrow?"

Bevin stared at him, astonished that he had simply agreed with her and made his statement. It was not how she expected him to react. Her father, the only man whom she had much contact with, would have argued and stalled until the matter was dropped. That wasn't right, Bevin knew.

"They would do that?"

"They would, sweetheart." Blaze reached for Bevin's hand and tugged her from the cabin and to his vehicle. He tucked her inside before he stood, looking around. Someone was out there, someone who meant them harm. He reached for Bevin's hand once he had seated himself in the vehicle. "It's who they are, sweetheart. They are always willing to speak of their stories, just to help others know that they are not alone and that God never forgets them. Ian, one of Abe's men, is known for offering to fly the couple away into hiding."

"He does that? Maybe we should do that. Only you can't leave." Bevin was sober as she spoke, knowing that Blaze just couldn't up and leave his charities. Nor would she ask that of him. "We need to talk to someone, Blaze, who understands what we are going through."

"We do. A retired forensics psychologist has offered to do that. Darci has spoken to others over time. I have reached out to her for help with others myself. She has always told me that if I or my lady needed to speak with her, that she would do that." Blaze parked near a favourite spot on the beach. "Wait here. I'll grab a meal for us and be right back. Lock the doors."

Blaze walked away towards the restaurant, knowing that he had been followed and deeply afraid for his lady. He nodded at an off-duty officer that he knew as the officer moved past him to stand near his vehicle and watch for anyone meaning them harm.

Bevin studied the man and sighed. It had to be an officer, she decided, and he just had to be out there, didn't he? Bevin was tired of not being able to live her life. She thought back over the years and frowned deeper. Something was off with her father and she needed to find out what. Only she didn't know how to find out that very fact. She was not sure that her mother would even know or would even speak with her.

Chapter 26

Walking along the hard-packed sand of the beach, Blaze tightened his hold on Bevin's hand. He was afraid of losing her now that he had found her. He didn't know if there was anyone out there that night. Blaze didn't have the sense that someone was watching them but he could very well be wrong.

Bevin looked out over the lake, seeing the shadow of the land in another country, a country that she had never traveled to or had any desire to do so. She looked up at Blaze, finding him distracted for a moment.

"Blaze?" Bevin's quiet voice reached through his thoughts and brought his attention to her. "How do we find out who it is?"

"That's a good question. Abe and Emma will help. For tonight, we have other decisions to make." He grinned down at the lady whom he loved so much.

"We do? Such as?" Bevin was puzzled for a moment before she frowned at him. "A wedding date?"

"Correct. I don't want to rush you but I'm hoping it's soon." Blaze bit at his lip, a sign of uncertainty.

"We can do that. How about next Friday?" Bevin grinned up at him, seeing that she had taken him by surprise. "Do we want to put it off and lose what time we may have as a married couple? We have no idea what we are still facing or how dangerous it may become. Only God sees that. I have not had the sense that He is saying no to our marriage."

"No, I haven't had that as well." He grinned down at her once more. "So, will you marry me next Friday?"

"I will. We just need to find a minister if ours isn't available." She looked up as he laughed. "Blaze?"

"He's already been in touch, asking when. He offered any day next weekend." Blaze hugged Bevin, a kiss dropped to the top of her head. "What all do we have left to plan?"

"I don't know if we have much to plan. We don't want many people there. You know who you want to ask. It's just my Mom, I think. I have no idea where Dad is at present. Sometimes, I wonder if he is involved in this and had gone into hiding."

"He may be but we don't know that. Okay. A small wedding. We'll work on a guest list but it won't hold many names. I promise you that." Blaze turned them back towards the parking lot. "We'll work on that over the next few days, sweetheart. For now, it's starting to get dark and I would like to be home and safe."

"I know, Blaze. I hate this. I hate living with restrictions on when and how we move. But if we don't, we might not live." Bevin had gone to the centre of the problem, how to stay safe.

Blaze paced his office that evening before he found a seat in an upholstered chair set into a corner by his bookshelves which were fully loaded with often read books. He frowned as he thought through the drive home. They had been followed, he knew, but he just didn't know if it was someone protecting them or after them. That was the question that no one seemed able to answer at the moment. Blaze feared for his lady and took that fear to his Abba Father. Hours later, his head raised and he rose, heading for a shower and clean clothes. It was early morning, he knew, squinting at the clock in the kitchen as he set the first of what would become many pots of coffee over the day. His friends would be stopping by as would Frank, he had no doubt. They were just not that close to finding out who. And Blaze suspected that Bevin was correct. Someone on his security teams had to be involved. He had asked the head of security to forward all the names on to Emma. That man had stared at Blaze for a moment before he nodded. It had to be done. They ran security checks every six months but they were not to the depth of what Emma would be able to perform.

The next morning, Blaze's hand tightened on Bevin's as they walked towards their church building. Both knew that they needed to be there, but they were afraid of what might occur to others.

"We can't live in fear, Blaze." Bevin hesitated for a moment before she walked through the doors.

"No, we can't. Security wants us at the back this morning." Blaze nodded at friends and acquaintances as he followed Bevin into a row of chairs and then sat, his had reaching for hers once more. He looked around, finding Darbi heading his way, her husband, Flynn, studying the people around them. They had been through what was generally termed as an adventure as had her sister, her two cousins, and her aunt. Darbi had been a good friend to him over the years.

"Blaze? May we join you?" Darbi's softly spoken question had Bevin jumping for a moment. She simply sat beside Bevin, reaching to hug her.

Bevin was taken aback, she thought, by the hug, realizing that Darbi was a good friend to Blaze from what he had said. Her attention went back to the activity on the stage at the front, losing herself in the simply worship for her Abba Father.

That afternoon, Bevin faced Blaze, struggling to keep the grin from her face. Blaze faced her, an open and wide grin on his face. He was up to no good, she decided, and didn't know if she really wanted to find out what it was.

"Come on, Bevin. We've been asked over to Ashlynn's for a meal. You know them. At least, I think that you do." Blaze finally reached for her hand to tug her away with him, Mary and Art watching with huge smiles on their faces.

"But do I want to go?" Bevin was being obstinate for a moment, not sure if she wanted to be around anyone and bring danger to them.

"We'll be fine. Torin will have taken steps to make it safe for us." Blaze tucked Bevin into his vehicle before he was behind the wheel and driving off. As he drove, his audible prayer filled the SUV, bringing Bevin's eyes to him.

———

138

Bevin simply shook her head. This was a side of Blaze that she had never seen and liked it. He just didn't do anything without praying over it first. He had told her that but she had not really believed him. This made her do that.

"Blaze? Where do we go with the investigation? Frank isn't saying much." Bevin stared out of the side window of the vehicle, her eyes taking in the scenery without registering that she was.

"I know, sweetheart. Torin asked me about that. He's willing to reach out to friends for us. He wanted to speak with us today, if you're up to it." Blaze grinned as she snorted, something he had come to expect from her at times.

"I am up to it. I want this over before the weekend. But I don't know that we can do that. I can feel danger moving in on us. And I just want to know who and why."

Neither couple saw the vehicle following them, keeping as close as it could. That vehicle sped past Blaze as he turned into Torin and Ashlynn's driveway, causing Bevin to stare after it.

Chapter 27

Ashlynn approached Bevin, not sure how to address the concerns that she had. It would not be Ashlynn if she didn't speak with a lady in distress.

Bevin turned as she heard footsteps approaching her. She had retreated to the back deck, finding the swing and sitting. She knew that she was likely being anti-social but for now, that was how she was.

"Bevin? What can we do for you?" Ashlynn simply sat beside her, waiting for the other lady to speak. She knew that Blaze planned to marry this lady, and she was glad for that. That would bring Bevin into the friend group, if that was what she wanted.

"What can you do for me? I am really not sure what you can do for me. Blaze has told me your stories or as much as he knows about them. How did you ever survive?" Bevin was puzzled by the fact that the lady sitting beside her went through something as did her four nieces. Their stories were almost unbelievable except Bevin knew that it was true.

"God. That is how we did it. God led us and protected us. He also had our friends involve themselves in our lives in a way that we were not expecting." Ashlynn rubbed at her face for a moment. "Frank almost died at one point from an assault involving one of my girls. Thank the Lord that he survived and returned to work. He is more cautious as he works, given that."

"I see." Bevin stared down the beautiful landscaped property, knowing that Ashlynn was not telling all that had happened. "How do we do this, Ashlynn? How do we keep moving forward and not failing at trusting God?"

"It's difficult to do that, Bevin. God is there everywhere we go. He doesn't allow anything to happen to us that is not in His will for us. He knew from before time began what you and Blaze would face. He protects you, covering you with His wings and with His hands. He hides you where you need to be hidden. That is not to say that bad things won't happen or that you won't be hurt. He doesn't wrap us in bubble wrap and stick us away somewhere. That is not the God who loves us and who we love and serve."

"I get that, Ashlynn. It's just so difficult to trust when you're facing things like this." Bevin looked up as she felt a hand on her and moved over to let Blaze sit beside her. She watched as Torin sat beside Ashlynn.

"Bevin? What are your biggest concerns?" Torin went right to the heart of the matter.

"My biggest concerns? That Blaze will be seriously injured or killed. That his family will be injured or disappear. His friends? The same. I fear for my Mom. Dad? I have no idea where he is at present or if he is even still in the province. Mom hasn't heard from him either. So, tell me. How do we do this?" Bevin felt Blaze's arm tighten around her. They had discussed this very topic earlier that morning.

"Those are all fair questions, Bevin. I think anyone who is going through what you are or has gone through it has asked them at some point. I know that Ashlynn and I did. We did what we could to keep everyone safe. Sometimes, that's not possible. It's taken out of our hands. That's when our faith and trust in God comes through." Torin shifted on his seat as he heard a sound from Blaze. "Blaze?"

"I have to agree with you, Torin. We've discussed this many times during and after what you and Ashlynn and what the girls went through. It's not an easy road we are sometimes asked to walk. I just remember that we were prayed for in the garden and that God has already walked this path and knows the outcome. We may not like what we have to go through, but we do go through it with our hands in each other's but more importantly in confidence that God does protect us and lead us." Blaze tilted his head to study his lady.

Bevin was not looking at any of them. Instead, her focus was on the yard and what was in it. She enjoyed gardening and was looking forward to putting her touch on Blaze's gardens. For now, she was enjoying the variety of flowers and shrubs and trees that made up Torin's.

"How do we find them, Ashlynn? How do we bring them out of the woodwork and to justice? I don't want to see anyone hurt but I know that can happen." Bevin finally turned her gaze towards the other couple, seeing them both nodding at her questions.

"Those are the questions that we all asked. The girls would be good for you to speak with. In fact, they asked me to question you whether you would join us for a Bible study and prayer time that we have with one another each week. They would welcome you. And Blaze, you are already part of the men's even though you haven't been able to be there recently." Ashlynn was on her feet, drawing Darbi into the conversation. "Darbi, you have been friends with Blaze for years as has your sister and also your cousins. You went through danger recently. What can you tell Bevin?"

Darbi studied her aunt and then studied Bevin. She didn't know the lady just because Bevin was not from their town but she knew that because of Blaze, they would need to get to know her. He would not tolerate anyone ignoring the lady whom he had chosen to share his life with.

"What can I tell her? It's tough going through this. It was hard watching the others go through their adventures, knowing that I had faced. All I can say is trust God even when it seems the darkest. He never walks away from you. He will never leave you or forsake you." Darbi was on her feet, her emotions still raw from what they had experienced. She didn't know how she could answer that question and provide any answers for someone else.

The two men had risen to their feet as Darbi ran from the deck, dismay on their faces. Seating themselves once more, they shared a look. It would be difficult, Blaze knew, to get any of the girls to speak with Bevin. And she desperately needed to hear others' stories.

Sighing, Blaze reached for his phone. It has been vibrating off and on for the last hour and he had been ignoring it. He squinted at the name and nodded. Emma Finlay was coming through. And that would certainly send the investigation forward. He just didn't know if they would like what she would have to say.

"Blaze?" Bevin's quiet voice roused him from the contemplation of what Emma may have found.

"It's okay. It's the friend, Emma, who has been trying to reach me. She and her husband, Abe, want to meet with us tomorrow night. We should. She'll have found information that we need. And any information that she has verified and confirmed will go to Frank. It's what she does." Blaze dropped a kiss on Bevin's temple, not seeing the speculative looks sent their way.

Chapter 28

Friday night arrived after what had seemed such a long week. Bevin had been out and about, not caring that she was being followed. It was what she fully expected, after all. Someone was after either her or Blaze but neither one of them had any idea why. That was concerning, but not as concerning as Bevin had expected. She had prayed about it and left it in her Father's hand.

Blaze paced the area in front of the fireplace in his cabin. To say he was nervous was an understatement. He was taking a step forward in life that he never expected to take, that of marrying the lady he loved and adored more than anyone else.

Bevin paused for a moment in the hallway, her eyes on Blaze. Frank's hand rested on the one of hers that curled around his arm. Her father had not appeared and they weren't able to track him down. That concerned Frank, a lot, as they were now coming to the conclusion that her father may well be part of what had happened. The evidence was leading that way.

"Okay, Bevin?" Frank's quiet question startled her for a moment before Bevin nodded.

"I am, Frank. Thank you for stepping in. You have proven what a true friend you are to both of us." She smiled sadly. "This was what Dad was to do. Only, he doesn't seem to care if he is in my life or Mom's life any more."

Moving forward at a subtle nudge from Frank, Bevin studied the knight waiting for her, a knight whom her mother had woven into her stories over the years. That lady had had a long talk with her daughter the day before and then just prayed for the couple.

Blaze moved through his house later that evening, greeting the friends and family who had gathered. He was on a search for his lady, knowing that they were cutting it close to leaving. They had not told anyone of their plans to simply head for a nearby cabin that Blaze owned and spend the weekend there.

Monday found Blaze once more in his office, a frown on his face as he listened to his secretary. Someone had tried hard to reach him over the weekend, calling numerous times and leaving confused and muddled messages. There was no clear reason given why this man had tried this many times.

"He didn't leave a name?" Blaze studied the messages that he was handed.

"Not once. I don't like this, Blaze. I already called the head of security and also Frank. They need to be in on what is discovered." She walked way, the door closing quietly behind her.

Blaze looked up an hour later as a tap came to his door and then it opened to reveal Frank. Frank looked angry, not at Blaze but at the situation.

"Blaze? How do we keep you safe? And then keep Bevin safe? These are threats, you know. I had our lab go over them and they could clean them up enough to hear what was being said."

"I gathered that you had." Blaze sank back in his black leather office chair. "I want this person."

"And we will get them. It is Bevin's father." Frank had not expected that and he was reading Blaze correctly in that he had not either.

"Her father? Why?" Blaze rubbed at his face. "I need to speak with Bevin."

"I have George bringing her here. We'll meet and discuss this. I don't think that she has expected this either."

Blaze was shaking his head. Bevin and he had discussed this already, that something like this might happen.

"You may be surprised, Frank. She was expecting something like this." Blaze was on his feet as he saw Bevin hesitating in the hallway, reaching for her and just wrapping her into his arms. "It's okay, sweetheart. We'll find your father."

"I know that we will. But which of us will be injured or even dead?" Bevin's hand was shaking as she held out an envelope. "I received this today. It's from him. He didn't sign it but I recognize his handwriting. Why does he hate me so much?" Bevin buried her head against her groom, sobs shaking her body.

Blaze gently picked her up and carried her into his office, his foot shutting the door behind them. Frank was on his feet, dismayed at the turn of events, taking the envelope from Bevin's shaking hand. Opening the letter, Frank drew in a sharp breath. No lady, young or old, should be subjected to the venom and hate that spewed from the written words. He walked from the office, intent on finding the man but knowing that it might not be possible at the moment.

Blaze sat, his lady cradled close to him. He looked up as his secretary entered and set a tray on his desk, nodding his thanks to her. She just seemed to know when tea and coffee were needed without being asked.

"Bevin? Frank has the letter. You are terrified, I can tell. What did your father threaten you with?" Blaze waited patiently for Bevin to compose herself and then speak.

"With just about anything you could think of. He threatened Mom, you, your parents, your friends, your company." Bevin looked up, her eyes dewy from her tears. "How do we stop him?"

"That's a good question. We can ask Emma to look into your father. In fact, I suspect that she already has." Blaze groaned as his phone chimed but he ignored it. Bevin was the most important person to him right then.

"We need to make some plans, Blaze, and how do we do that when we don't even know where he is?" Bevin chewed at her bottom lip, not realizing that she was. Her eyes studied the office that held her husband's work. "Who decorated your office?"

Blaze stared at her for a moment before he shook his head. She must have a reason for asking.

"Mom did with Mary's help. Why?"

"Because there is something off in here. I didn't feel it when we were here last week. Today, I do." Bevin was on her feet, heading for the security team who were waiting down the hall. "Fellows? We need to search Blaze's office. Something is off in there."

Blaze stood and stared at Bevin before he looked up, nodding as the team moved his way.

"She's right. For now, we need to search my office and any area that I may frequent. Just to be on the safe side. If Bevin says something is off in here, then there is." Blaze reached for his phone, tucking it into a pocket, and then reached for Bevin's hand, walking with her towards the building cafeteria. A cup of tea or coffee would be good about now, he thought, seeing as they didn't get to enjoy the ones that were now sitting and cold on his desk.

Chapter 29

Frank walked back towards Blaze, watching him as he stood outside of his building. He was angry once more. Someone had managed to breach the heavy security that Blaze had established in his building and plant devices in Blaze's office. Bevin was good, he thought, to have picked up on that.

"Frank?" Blaze's voice cut through the dark thoughts that Frank was trying hard to avoid.

"Blaze? Bevin was correct. We did find devices in your office and in the waiting room. We've removed them. I just don't understand who."

"Nor do I. We've been going back over everything for years now, the lawyers and I, and can't come up with any names for you. And we should be able to." Blaze was frustrated at that. At least if they could come up with some names, they would have something for Frank to investigate.

Frank nodded. That was the case, he knew. Blaze just didn't seem to make enemies but someone hated him enough to cause all these problems for him. And Bevin seemed to be involved in some way that they could not trace. She still had not been able to answer why she ended up in their town and at Blaze's office building.

That night, Blaze wrapped an arm around Bevin and guided her to the couch in the living room. They were still in the other cabin, deciding to stay there for a couple of weeks, hoping to throw off anyone who was looking for them. Besides, it offered them privacy that they craved.

"Where do we stand with the investigation, Blaze? Did Frank say?" Bevin's head went down against her groom's shoulder.

"No, he hasn't said. So far, I don't know that he has anyone whom he is investigating. We just don't have the names. And Emma hasn't been able to find out anything either." Blaze was discouraged and frustrated as well as being scared. He didn't want anything to happen to his lady and that was a real possibility, he knew.

"So, how do we find them?" Bevin was quite willing to put herself out there in the hopes of trapping one of the man. And in trapping one of the men, she was praying that he would talk and tell who was after them. Only, she didn't think that it would work. "I like this cabin, Blaze. I know the other one is your home and I do like it, but this one is more home and more you."

"Is it?" Blaze looked around at the simplicity that he had incorporated into it. "I think that you are right. With Mary and Art on site, it is home but not a home that provides solitude. This one does. Is there a reason you're mentioning this?" Blaze waited for Bevin to sort out her thoughts. He had learned that she needed time to do just that with big questions.

Bevin shrugged. She had no idea why she felt that way.

"I can't really say, Blaze. I love your home but at times, I need to be away from people. I don't know that I can over there." She looked up at him, seeing his understanding of her words on his face. "I don't know that I'm making any sense."

"You are, sweetheart. You are. I feel the same way. We can live between the two, if that's what you want. Mary and Art wouldn't be offended, if that's what you think. Art approached me last week, simply stating that they would find another place to live, if that was what we wanted."

"Oh, we can't kick them out of their home!" Bevin was horrified at the thought.

"We wouldn't be. There is a small home just behind the cabin that they would use. They have often asked if that's what I want. I have always said no, there wasn't any need for me to be on my own. Now, there is, and they are willing to move there." Blaze hugged Bevin tighter. "We'll leave that discussion for now. Tonight? We'll spend time in prayer and silence before our God. That's what we need."

Bevin agreed with him. They did need that time with God. She feared for what was coming, for the unseen enemy, for the unknown danger that they faced. No one person could tell them how to prepare for that.

Raising her head early the next morning, Bevin listened carefully. She was sure that she heard noise outside of the cabin, the noise made by men trying to get it. Instead, it was the wind, she decided, snuggling closer to Blaze and finding his arm tightening around her. She slept, not knowing that they had been found and that the danger awaiting them would test their faith and their love for each other.

<hr>

Blaze was on his feet earlier than he had expected. Dressing quickly, he reached for the heavy walking stick that he had left by the back door and then unlocked the door. He hesitated for a moment before he was out of the cabin and stalking around it. It was as Blaze had expected. Someone had been around the cabin during the night. He sighed. This was not how he expected his first week of married life to be. He walked back towards the house, stopping as he saw the two men waiting for him. This was not how his day was to start, Blaze decided, standing exactly where he had stopped. There was no way that he was moving forward and approaching them. If they wanted him, they had to approach him.

Bevin stood out of sight in the kitchen, her eyes on Blaze before she was moving silently away and reaching for her phone. A quick call to the authorities had a promise that they would be there as soon as they could. Where could Bevin hide herself to stay safe? She snorted at that. There was no way that she was hiding and leaving Blaze to face the two men. Then, her head dropped. That would be exactly what he would expect her to do.

Spinning in a circle, Bevin tried hard to remember what Blaze had said and where she could hide. She ran for the laundry area, her hands feeling along the wall until she found the switch that moved the wall towards her. She ducked inside, pulling the wall closed and then crouched on the steps that led to the hiding place under the stairs. There was no way that she was heading that way, not without Blaze. And she had no idea if Blaze would be around for her to head down the stairs with.

Blaze refused to move despite the commands of the men. One of them, frustrated at Blaze's refusal, stalked towards him, a weapon trained on him. Blaze's face remained blank, despite the fear or terror that he felt. He had no idea if Bevin was safe. All he could do was pray that she was. God was in control, despite what the men in front of him had decided.

Forced to walk away from the cabin, Blaze kept his face neutral no matter how much he feared for his beloved Bevin. He had no idea where he was heading. The men weren't talking, and he wasn't about to ask.

Chapter 30

Frank paced the area around the cabin, taking care to stay away from the footprints. He could tell that Blaze was one of the men who had walked away. He just feared for him and also for Bevin. There was no sign that Bevin had been there, outside, when Blaze disappeared.

Walking through the house, Frank frowned. A remembered thought had him heading for the laundry room. At one time, Blaze had shown him the hiding place. They had talked about it, wondering how long it had been there. The cabin had been renovated when Blaze had purchased it, with him simply changing out appliances, flooring, and paint colours, other than renewing the fixtures in the bathroom.

Frank felt along the wall, finding the switch and pulling the panel open. A soft sound had him reaching inside and finding an arm. A gentle tug on his hand elicited a sob as Bevin erupted from the hiding place.

"Frank? What?" Bevin stared at him before she was running towards the outdoors and searching for Blaze. "Where is Blaze?"

George stopped her headlong rush to find Blaze by simply wrapping her into his arms and then literally carrying her back to the deck where he stood her on her feet, not releasing her. He shared a look with Frank who was shaking his head.

"Bevin? What can you tell us?" Frank's repeated questions finally reached through the dullness that had overtaken Bevin.

Bevin spun to stare at him. Blaze was missing and Frank and George didn't seem to be searching for him.

"Where is Blaze? I have no idea what happened. There were two men out here with him. I ran to hide as he had told me to do if something like this happened. I did what he wanted." Bevin shoved away from George to stand and stare at the yard where activity was occurring. She recognized the fact that she could not go down there as much as she wanted to search for Blaze. "He was out here. I saw him. He looked at me and I knew that I had to hide. And no, I can't describe the men to you. I was focused on Blaze and then finding the hiding spot." Bevin glared at Frank as he smiled at her for a moment. "How did you know where it was?"

"Blaze showed me one day. I am glad that I did. That meant I could find you right away." Frank's hand on her arm drew her away from the deck and back into the house. "We'll stay in here for a bit, Bevin. Then, we'll need to move you somewhere safer." Frank stared at Bevin for a moment as she glared at him.

"I am going nowhere other than here. This is the home that Blaze and I have chosen for now. He would expect to find me here." Bevin walked or almost ran from Frank, a door closing softly behind her.

Frank's head dropped. This was not how Bevin was to react. She was to cooperate with him and go with him to a safe space. Obviously, that would not be happening. A sudden thought had him on the move, searching the house for Bevin. The door that had closed had been to the office. Opening it, Frank found what he expected. Right now, Frank had other places that he needed to be, including the office to start the search for Blaze. A quiet few words with George had George nodding and then heading around the cabin to begin a search for Bevin. Neither man expected her to hide for long. They were greatly disappointed in that supposition. Bevin had hidden herself and hidden herself well. Lessons learned as a child were coming back to her.

Blaze's parents were shocked to hear that their son was missing. Emily was certain that Frank was wrong, that Blaze had simply disappeared and would reappear later that morning. She walked away, heading for Bevin, not finding that young lady. Brenna had appeared as well to search for her daughter.

"Where would she hide, Emily?" Brenna studied the cabin and then the surrounding forest.

"Somewhere in the forest. Blaze had many hiding spots around here as a youngster. I have no idea where they are nor does Brody. He never caused us to worry about him." Emily rubbed at her upper arms. "We're being watched and not by someone who wants to help us."

Brody had appeared at that point, watching the forest. He could sense the danger that was awaiting them before he herded the ladies back to his truck and into it. He didn't want to drive away from where his son had last been seen but he had no choice. Frank was working it. Friends were out with flyers and searching for Blaze. His security team was doing the same.

Emma had reached out to Brody, concerned about the couple. When she heard that Blaze was missing, she simply went to Abe and asked that the team search. He had been glad to do that, calling in two other search teams run by friends of his, Richard and Don. They would find Blaze, that they were certain of. Emma was working away, trying to determine just where he might be. They were concerned for Bevin, hearing that she had just walked away from the cabin. That deed might mean her death, they decided, and they needed to find her.

Abe's team headed for the forest around the cabin, moving quietly but quickly through the underbrush. They found Bevin's trail and tracked her, not seeing her as they did so.

"Where is she, Abe?" Murphy spoke quietly. "She has to be here somewhere. These are her tracks we're following, aren't they?"

"They are. She's trying hard to stay hidden and that makes it dangerous for her." A sudden abrupt sound had the two men spinning before they moved rapidly towards the sound.

Matt, the paramedic on the team, was on his knees beside Bevin, assessing her. She was in a crumpled heap of lady on the trail, not rousing as Matt's hands gently assessed her. He looked up, shaking his head at Abe.

"She's not hurt, not that I can see or assess, Abe." Matt rose, a hand rubbing at his cheek. He stared around the area, seeing nothing that would have caused her to collapse.

"Okay. Let's get her back to the cabin and then to the hospital. Her family and Blaze's family need her. Frank would also likely want to speak with her." Abe watched with compassion as Matt gently gathered her into his arms and turned to walk towards the cabin, finding himself in the centre of the group of men. It was what they did to protect anyone.

Frank turned from his desk as he heard George's voice. He frowned. George had been at the cabin and then heading for Mary and Art. Why was he here?

George had come to a stop at Frank's office door. He was out of breath from running.

"Frank? Abe's team moved in a while ago. Abe called. They have Bevin and are heading for the hospital with her."

Frank was on his feet and heading for the door, swinging it shut behind him and locking it.

"How is Bevin?" He shot George a look when George didn't answer. "George? How is she?"

"Abe said that she was unconscious but didn't seem harmed. Matt, their paramedic, did a preliminary assessment." George fastened his seatbelt at Frank took off from the curb in front of the station. "I sent someone to find the parents." He frowned. "Where is her father?"

"That we don't know. He's around here somewhere, I would suspect. He's just hiding from us all." Frank parked near the emergency entrance.

"Before we go in, let's pray, George. This is getting worse for them. Bevin will want to be out there searching and we can't stop her. All we can do is ensure that she has someone with her."

"And that is going to be difficult to do, I would imagine. She's not one to sit back and wait." George walked beside Frank into the hospital, nodding as Frank pointed towards the waiting room. He would head there and be with the families. He knew that security from Blaze's company as well as patrol officers would be out there, watching out for Blaze's beloved Bevin and their families.

Chapter 31

Rousing slightly, Bevin listened to the quiet sounds around her. She sighed. She hadn't been successful after all in hiding. Bevin had gone as far as she could before despair had driven her to her knees. She had collapsed, sobs shaking her body before she could sob no more. Bevin had given up, despairing of ever seeing Blaze once more. She just knew that the next time that she saw him, he would be dead. Her despair was at the point where she couldn't even pray or acknowledge that God was in control.

Rising from the stretcher, Bevin crept to the door, peeking out. It was as she suspected. An officer was at her door. Watching until his head turned the other way, Bevin quickly moved out among the nurses and other staff who were in the hallway.

Frank stood in her doorway, a sigh rising from him. She had to do that, didn't she? Run away again and without anyone seeing her. The officer had been shocked to see that the room was empty. He denied seeing her leave and Frank believed him. Now, he had to track her down, and he had no idea how to do that.

Bevin crept from the hospital, her head moving as she searched for anyone after her. A small scream came from her as she ran into a tall man watching her. Torin had appeared at the request of Ashlynn.

"Bevin? Escaping, are we?" Torin grinned at her before his hand was under her elbow and directing her to his truck. "In we go. Ashlynn suspected that you might try and escape the security around you.

Don't ask how she knew. She just did." Torin drove away, a hand raised to George who stood and stared after him. "George saw me but I don't know that he knows it was you. You will have to let them know."

"I know. I will at some point. Frank will know that I ran." Bevin struggled to control her emotions. "I don't know what to do or where to go, Torin."

"Come to Ashlynn, Bevin. She's ready to help you. You need someone with you, and somehow I don't think you want your mother or Blaze's parents near you at the moment."

"No, I don't." Bevin had her phone out, sending out text messages to those people just stating that she was fine and with friends. She would call them later and begging them to pray that Blaze came home safe and sound.

Ashlynn waited just inside the open front door as she watched Torin aid Bevin her way. Bevin's steps were slow and staggered at the moment. She felt it hard to keep her balance.

Bevin looked up as she approached the steps, not sure how she would ever mount them. One by one, she climbed, her steps stopping on each stair. Torin kept a hand under her arm to balance her, his gaze moving from Bevin to Ashlynn.

Ashlynn moved to hug Bevin once that lady was inside the house.

"You're tired and worried and scared, Bevin. It's normal to feel that way. Come with me. You can get cleaned up and we'll find something easy for you to eat." Ashlynn closed the bedroom door behind Bevin, knowing that she had left clothes for that lady. She walked quickly through the house to the kitchen, finding Torin waiting for her as she walked into his hug. "What happened?"

"Blaze disappeared. Bevin had hidden herself away before Frank found her. She ran on him and he couldn't find her. Abe's team moved in. She was out of it when Matt assessed her. Bevin then ran from the hospital. You were right to send me there. She was just standing, looking lost and alone." Torin sighed. "We'll need to reach out to their folks."

"No, we let her do that. She needs some kind of control over her life right now. That's not happening. With Blaze disappearing, she's lost the compass to what is keeping her sane and moving. We'll help her, won't we?" Ashlynn stared up at Torin, seeing his nod.

"We can't do anything less than that, sweetheart. Blaze helped us without us knowing it at the time. He doesn't do that for anything in response. But we will work with whoever it is that we need to. He needs to come home." Torin looked towards the hallway, hearing footsteps coming their way. "Bevin needs to hear the girls' stories."

"She does and she will. We didn't go into them that day but I am sure that the girls will all come around. We just can't overwhelm her." Ashlynn turned to find Bevin hesitating in the doorway. "Bevin? What can we get for you? Other than to find Blaze."

Bevin drew in a deep quivering breath. That was all she wanted, to have Blaze back home and safe. She had no idea who the two men were or where he had been taken. She needed to research them. Only, Bevin wasn't quite sure on how to do that.

"Emma is looking for Blaze, Bevin." Torin's hand once more drew her forward and to a seat at the kitchen table. "For now, Ashlynn has a light meal for us. We'll eat, as best as we can, and then spend time in prayer. It's what Blaze would want."

"I know that it is. I just don't know if I can eat. How did you two ever do it? And your girls, Ashlynn?" Bevin reached for the sandwich on the plate in front of her and ate without even being aware that was what she was doing.

"It was hard, Bevin. I can't deny it. For all four girls to face danger as they did and then myself? It took a lot from us. And it was hard knowing that the girls' parents had been murdered and that someone was after me and using the girls to do that. It was tough. God got us through." Ashlynn wiped at a tear that had escaped. Even now, so many months after what the girls had faced, it troubled her and caused her grief.

Bevin listened carefully to the stories of the five ladies. She had not been aware that they were so devastating, particularly where Ashlynn's brothers and their wives were concerned.

"How did you ever do it, Ashlynn? You were young when you took on the girls and then faced this later. I don't know if I could have done that." Bevin was horrified to put it lightly at what they had faced.

"It's not what we chose or how we wanted to live. I grieved for my brothers for myself and also for the girls. They needed their parents and didn't have them. But you asked how we did it. It was God, Bevin, His strength, His peace, His love, His protection, His defense. Without Him, we would have not made it. I am sure that at some point, we would have tried suicide. But He worked it all out for His glory and honour. He was our Avenger and Defender. He will be yours. I have no idea what you will face or how you will face it. I have no idea where Blaze is at present." Ashlynn gave a quick grin. "Do you know how he got his nickname?"

Bevin stared at the other lady for a moment. She had no idea and stated as much.

"Darbi likes to tell the story and she tells it much better that I do. When they were young, Darbi around twelve, I think, Blaze became friends with the girls at school. Because they were orphans, they took a lot of flak from other students. David as he was known at the time didn't like that. Darbi said one day it was as if a match had been lit under him and he took on the ringleader. Of course, he did have to pay the consequences of that act. But he had no regrets of tackling that student and making him aware of just how the girls were suffering. That boy became a friend to the girls. His name? George. He's the investigator working with Frank. As to the nickname, everyone said it was if a match had been struck and blazed quickly. That was how they described Blaze's reaction. After that, no one dared ignite his wrath. And he became known as Blaze. Now, his reactions are still to help others but the blaze of his work is hidden from most people. Only those nearest and dearest to him know what he does and who he is."

Chapter 32

Bevin wandered the cabin that night, a sober look on her face. She had appreciated Torin and Ashlynn spending time with her. She just felt as if she was bringing danger to everyone. Frank had tracked her down but she had refused to speak with him, shutting the door in his face. That man had shaken his head before he walked away. She would speak with him and do that on the next day.

Sitting in the chair that Blaze had seemed to favour brought him closer to her. She missed the tall handsome man who was her groom. All she could do was pray for him and beg God to bring him home. Towards morning, her prayers changed as she let go of her dream of him coming home. Bevin had to acknowledge that God was in control and it was His will that would bring Blaze back to them. They just might not like how he came back.

A tap at the back door had Bevin on her feet a few hours later. A hand covered her mouth to still the scream that gathered in her throat. Tiptoeing through the cabin, Bevin carefully studied the door and then the person behind it. It was Brody. She reached to unlock the door and let him in. Brody simply hugged her and then stood with his hands on her arms.

"Bevin? You've been here alone." Brody didn't need to ask.

"I have been, Brody. I have been. I spent the night in prayer." Bevin blinked rapidly to stop the tears from falling. Brody was acting as her own father should and wasn't.

"That's what we wondered. We didn't want to come in overnight." Brody turned for a moment, staring at the back door. "What can we do for you?"

"What can you do for me?" Bevin gave a harsh laugh as she paced the openness of the cabin. She liked that there were no hallways to get lost in. Blaze had just laughed at her when she said that.

"Yes. What can we do for you?" Brody stepped into her path and stopped her.

"I don't know. I should be the one asking what I can do for you." Bevin drew in a deep quivering breath. "How do we do this, Brody? How do we find him?"

"That's what we're planning on working through today. Come. Grab what you need for the day and we'll head for the other cabin." Brody gave a quick grin as she scowled at him for a moment. "It's your home, Bevin. If you don't want us working there, we'll find somewhere else to work."

"No, it's not that. It's just that Blaze disappeared from here. I'm afraid that he won't find me if I leave." Bevin had to finally admit to herself and Brody her deepest fear.

"He'll find you, Bevin. If he comes back today, he'll find you. He'll know that we are with you." Brody tucked Bevin into his truck, locking the cabin doors behind them. He was afraid for the young lady who had become part of their lives, afraid that she too would disappear and no one would ever find his son and his beloved bride.

Emily turned as she heard a door open and close and then soft footprints heading her way. She reached for Bevin, simply wrapping her into a mother hug. Brenna had not appeared as yet and that concerned Blaze's parents. They had reached out by phone and by text message with no answer from that lady.

"Where's Mom?" Bevin searched for her. "She's not here? What has he done with her?"

Brody and Emily stopped moving as they heard her words. Sharing a look, Emily moved towards Bevin.

"Why would you ask it like that, Bevin?"

"I don't know. Dad's changed. I think that he would keep Mom away from me." Bevin walked away from them, heading for the office and the piles of paper that seemed to have accumulated. She was soon immersed in reading through them, struggling to understand. Her note pad became to fill with thoughts and questions.

Emily watched her for a while before she sighed. They had friends heading that way over the day, including Torin and Ashlynn and their girls. Garrett, Brinn's father-in-law and a private investigator, had been working on something since Blaze had saved Bevin and wanted to speak with that lady. They couldn't say no, not if it meant their son coming home.

Frank stood at the office door an hour later, dressed casually. He was off that day and had tracked down Bevin. He was there as a friend, his wife, Sue, with him. Frank really did need to speak with the younger lady about what had happened to her, to further clarify what statement she had been able to give.

Bevin knew full well that Frank was standing there, watching her and waiting for her to look up. When she didn't, she heard his footsteps moving into the room before he sat in front of the desk. He would simply wait for Bevin to acknowledge him, if she ever did.

"Frank? I don't understand what this all means." Bevin finally looked at him, a sober and somber look to her face. She stared around the office, taking in the bookshelves, the pictures, and the furnishings. It was an office that was comfortable yet functional, an office where anyone could work.

"What don't you understand?" Frank was on his feet and around the desk, gently taking the papers from her hands. He read through it. "This? This is what our friend, Emma, has found. It's her investigation into the security team around Blaze. So far, she has not found one of them who would want to harm Blaze or you." Frank perched on the corner of the desk, watching Bevin. "Bevin, go back in time for me. What brought you to Grasspoint? I don't know if we ever asked that."

"What brought me here? I was running for my life, I guess. I knew that I had been followed and didn't know who to turn to or trust. I gave up my work and just ran." Bevin sighed, a deep from the toes sigh. "I still have to close out my apartment there. Blaze and I were going to do that this coming weekend."

"You can still do that. We'll work with you on that. His security team will be with you. Or we have friends who have security teams who would gladly do it as well. In fact, that's not a bad idea. They have all had adventures and would gladly share with you what they went through and how God protected and provided for them."

Bevin nodded, her thoughts not quite on what Frank was saying. Her hand shook as she offered him a piece of paper.

"What is this, Frank? Who is this person? Blaze has never been married or even dated. So why is she saying all this?" Fear shone out of Bevin's eyes.

Frank frowned at her before he took the paper and read it. He sighed to himself, something that he felt he had been doing a lot of lately.

"This person? She has a habit of doing this, claiming to be the girlfriend or wife of the young men in town. They all avoid her. I know for a fact that Blaze took out a restraining order against her that is still in effect. She should not be contacting him and she has." Frank's phone was out as he walked away, speaking with George and simply asking him to find the woman and bring her in for violating the restraining order. George was not surprised at that.

Frank turned to where he could watch Bevin once more. She was concentrating on the paperwork before she reached for the computer. He frowned, not sure what she was up to but allowed her the privacy that she needed to work away. His head turned as he felt someone beside him.

Torin watched Bevin as well.

"What is she up to?"

"I don't know but I know that she is determined to end this today if she can. I would not be surprised to find that the investigation that they're doing moves ahead quicker than ours does." Frank walked away, finding Sue and then finding Brody. "What can we do for her?"

"Nothing that I know of, Frank. She has to work through this on her own." Brody was saddened at the turn of events. He wanted his son home for their sakes but more so for Bevin.

Chapter 33

Late that night, Bevin stared at the text message on her phone. It had come from Blaze's phone but it didn't sound like him. He would not be asking her to meet him and alone, not while he was a captive somewhere. She sighed as she forwarded the message on to both Frank and George. Bevin didn't know if they had made any progress that day but the others seemed to think so.

Finding a blanket, Bevin wrapped it around herself and curled up in a chair, her head resting on the back of it. She couldn't pray, couldn't even think really. It had all become too much for her. The head of Blaze's security team had been in touch, just asking what they could do for her. She had simply replied that she didn't know. The only thing that she wanted was Blaze back home and that didn't appear to be happening anytime soon.

The next morning, Bevin was on her feet and heading for her car. She had had enough of sitting around, she decided. Today, she was heading for the next town and her apartment, ready to pack it up and clean it out. It was a furnished apartment that she had rented. And she really didn't have a lot of things, mostly just dress clothes and books.

Three hours later, Bevin closed the trunk of her car. She was done in this town, she decided, her life now in Grasspoint with Blaze. She didn't see the men in the truck watching her and then watching for anyone coming to help her. They were under orders to kidnap her as soon as they could. Blaze was not cooperating in the way that he should. Their employer felt that if Bevin was there and threatened in front of Blaze, he would cooperate. That man didn't understand the integrity that the couple had.

Frank walked towards Bevin, startling her for a moment. He smiled as she frowned at him.

"Bevin? We would have come with you and helped. I heard from an officer here that you were cleaning out your apartment." Frank rested a hand on the car trunk, knowing that he was too late to offer help.

"I had to, Frank. I just had to." Bevin stared around her, feeling unsettled. "Someone is out here."

"And there is. That's why we wanted to come with you." Frank pointed to the passenger side of the car even as he reached to gently take her keys from her hand. "In you go. George is here and dropped me off. We also have a friend with us. We'll get you home safely."

Bevin stared at the officer in front of her. She had not even considered the danger that she was in, she had been that focused on getting to the apartment and clearing it out.

"I'm sorry. I made extra work for you." Bevin fastened her seat belt, watching around but not seeing anyone who would cause her harm.

"We are all worried about you, Bevin, for your sake and for Blaze's. If they can use you to force Blaze to do something illegal, then his company and charities

are worthless. And we think that is why he was taken."
Frank pulled out onto the highway, seeing the cars that
surrounded him. He thanked God for friends who
stepped in to provide that assistance.

"I understand that, Frank. I know that they are
just waiting for me to slip up and be vulnerable enough
for them to do that. God is protecting me. I just don't
know where to turn for physical help." Bevin didn't
look at him, intent on the scenery flying by the car.

"We get that as well, Bevin. Work with us. I
have some friends from another town who would like
to speak with you. Simon and Blackie are in town right
now with their wives. Blackie's father, Samuel, has
been digging into this and has sent the two men to
speak with you." Frank pulled to a stop in front of the
cabin, reaching to stop Bevin from getting out of the
car. "Let me walk around your home and then inside
it, just to ensure that it's safe."

Frank was gone before he saw the horrified and
terrified look on Bevin's face. That fact had hit home
for once, and she knew then that she had to go on the
offensive. But she just did not know how to do that.
Perhaps these friends whom Frank had mentioned
would have some ideas for her.

Simon and Eavan and Blackie and Julia walked
towards Frank, finding him just standing and staring
around. Frank was uneasy about Bevin being at that
cabin but he could not persuade her to move elsewhere.
She had simply stated that was where Blaze had
disappeared from and where he would return to. Frank
just didn't understand her reasoning.

———

"Frank?" Simon stopped beside the man. "Where's Bevin?"

"In the cabin, I suspect, putting her things away. She is refusing to leave here." Frank's frustration at that came through.

"Can't say as I blame her." Blackie turned in a circle. "So far, has she been safe here?"

"She has been. She hasn't indicated if she has felt threatened her, but that can change. Come on. Let me introduce you to her and then I have to run." Frank was as good as his words, leaving Bevin staring at the two couples before she shrugged.

"Frank said that you can help?" Bevin reached for the coffee pot, intent on pouring them all coffees before the pot was removed from her hand. Simon shook his head at her for a moment before he proceeded to complete that task.

"Where can we meet, Bevin?" Blackie's words drew Bevin back to the room and from her troubling thoughts.

"The office, I guess." Bevin hesitated. "We should be meeting at the other cabin but I can't leave here."

"We get that, Bevin. We both had adventures which almost killed Simon and Eavan." Blackie's hand on her back directed her to the office. "We'll pray with you and then share our stories. They're not pretty."

"I don't imagine that they would be." Bevin sank gratefully into a chair, knowing that she was the peak of her discouragement and needed to have that prayer time, even with these couples who were strangers yet friends.

Blackie raised his head at last, assessing Bevin. He nodded to himself. She was stressed and struggling but moving forward as she could. He simply told his and Julia's story, the stories of two of their friends, and then let Simon tell their story.

Bevin stared at them, in shock for a moment, before her eyes closed. She was not alone, not as she had suspected. There were others out there who could somewhat understand what she was going through.

"So, how would you do this? What would you be looking for?" Bevin's questions didn't surprise them.

Blackie handed over the paperwork that they and his father had amassed. Bevin stared at it, stared at him, and then began to read, reaching for a pen at one point. She sat back once she had read it, a serious look on her face.

"You found all this? This person you name? You think they're the ones?" Bevin turned to Blackie, hope in her eyes that just maybe they would solve this and bring Blaze home.

"We do. He's been instrumental in crime in this town and has been reaching out. Your last town? He was there. For some reason, he fixated on you. We have confirmation of that. We just don't know why. That's we're working on as is our friend, Emma. She and Abe plan on coming over in a couple of days. She will have information that will move this ahead. And

Abe will have plans for you that will keep you as safe as we can. Nothing that we do is totally guaranteed. That's how life works." Simon paused for a moment, a frown crossing his face. "You do need to stay safe, Bevin, and that means listening to Frank and the others who are concerned about you." He grinned at the look on her face.

"I know that, Simon. I just don't have to like it. But if I don't do what they ask and advise, I may not survive and Blaze may not survive. I couldn't handle it if he was injured or killed because I didn't do what was asked of me." Bevin sat back in her chair, not seeing the looks the others were exchanging. "I've been praying for him to come home. Only, it doesn't seem as if my prayers are being answered."

Julia reached to hug Bevin.

"It seems that way but God is listening to you. We forget that whatever happens is in His will and His timing. It's hard, as humans, to wait and trust."

Chapter 34

Bevin raised her head from her pillow that night, frowning. She was certain that she heard someone in the cabin. On her feet, she reached for her clothes and dressed, hesitating to leave the bedroom, not sure if her hearing had been correct.

Drawing in a deep breath, Bevin reached for the door knob and slowly turned it, pulling the door towards her. She hesitated before she crept from the bedroom, her senses alert, her head turning as she moved towards the living room. Pausing, she frowned. There was someone in the cabin, of that she was now certain. She sighed. She had left her phone on the bedside table and would now need to retreat to retrieve it. Bevin just didn't know if she would have time to do that.

A dark shape approached her, the walk slow and hesitant before she was wrapped in familiar arms. A sob rose from within her as she heard Blaze's beloved voice simply stating her name. Her own arms came around him as she sobbed, not sure how he had gotten back to her but he was here.

Blaze staggered sideways slightly as he fought to keep his balance. All he knew was that he was free and at home with his beloved bride. He needed to talk with her but he also needed sleep even more.

Bevin leaned back to study Blaze, seeing the fatigue and stress that lined his face. She simply turned him back to the bedroom and to the shower, finding clean clothing for him. As the door closed to the bathroom, sobs choked her throat before Bevin was away, knowing that Blaze would not sleep right away. A pot of coffee was started as she shoved bread into the toaster. He needed something simple to eat, she decided.

Hearing soft footsteps behind her, Bevin turned to be once more wrapped in Blaze's arms. She couldn't control her sobs this time and felt his body shaking as well as he wept. They finally looked at one another before Blaze kissed her.

"You're okay, sweetheart?" Blaze had been terrified by the threats shouted at him regarding her. He had no idea how he had managed to keep calm and keep his emotions under check during the time that he had been held captive. Only God had been able to control them. That had been his prayer. The men had been waiting for Blaze to crack and acknowledge that he was in their control. That had never happened. He had no idea how he had become free that night but he knew that someone had helped him. And that someone had worked for his abductor.

Bevin finally convinced Blaze that he needed to sleep, but he refused to go to bed. Instead, he wrapped her into his arms as he sank down on the couch, not willing to let her go. She watched as he drifted off, the lines in his face easing somewhat. They needed to talk, but she also needed to let someone know that he was home. The only thing was that Blaze was not letting go of her. His arms relaxed enough at last that Bevin could rise.

Bevin stood and stared at her groom, puzzlement on her face. She had no idea how he managed to get free or if he was released. She sighed. He would have answers for her. Bevin just wasn't sure that she would like the answers that she would receive.

An hour later, Bevin stood once more and watched Blaze. He was deep into sleep, seeming to relax even more as he slept. She dropped a kiss on his cheek before she walked away to find her phone. Her hand turned it over and over on the kitchen counter as she stared out of the window, not seeing the awakening of the world that morning or the gorgeous pinks and purples of the rising sun. Bevin's thoughts were troubled. She needed to reach out to Frank. She just didn't want to. She wanted to keep the fact that Blaze was free and at home with her to herself. Only that wasn't fair to anyone else.

Her thoughts turned to prayers as she turned her head, listening for Blaze to be on his feet. He still slept, she thought, before her fingers found the keyboard on her phone. A simple text to Frank that read "he's home" was all that she sent. She could call his parents in a bit, Bevin decided. They deserved to hear her voice letting them know that their son was once more home. When that happened, Bevin was well aware that her home would become busy. She just wasn't sure that she was ready for that.

A quiet tap at the back door had Bevin jumping in fear. She crept that way, peeking around to see Frank standing there. His back was to the door as he surveyed the area around him, not seeing anything out of the ordinary. He turned back as Bevin opened the door, slipping in quietly and locking the door behind him. Frank gave Bevin a quick hug before he stood back, assessing her.

"When?" Frank only asked the one question, knowing that he had more but Bevin wasn't ready for them as of yet.

"Around two, I think. I heard someone in the house and went to investigate." Bevin glared at Frank as he frowned at her. "What else was I to do? I found Blaze heading my way. He hasn't said anything at all. In fact, he's been too quiet. He's been asleep since about three or so. I have no idea where he came from or where he's been."

"It's okay, Bevin. Here. Sit. You likely have been pacing for the last while." Frank grinned at her for a moment as he reached to make fresh coffee. "We'll talk, Bevin. But right now, let me pray with you. You two are not finished your adventure, not by a long shot. Blaze is home but he is still not safe. And because he is home, you are not safe. I can't answer for his parents as to their safety."

Frank was on his feet as he heard a noise at the front door, walking that way. He was not surprised to see Brody and Emily and even Brenna appearing as the door opened. They all frowned at him before they looked past him at Bevin.

Brenna drew in a deep breath and then wrapped her daughter in her arms. Something had changed overnight and she had a good idea that Blaze was home.

Emily hugged her as did Brody before Brody stood in front of her, his hands on her upper arms. It seemed as if that was all that was holding her on her feet.

"Blaze? He's home?" Brody had a good suspicion that was why he had been awakened so early in the morning and had a strong sense that he needed to be at his son's home.

Bevin nodded, hardly able to contain her tears.

"He is. He came home around two. Right now, he's asleep on the couch." Bevin stepped backwards as the three parents moved forward to stare at Blaze as he slept.

"He'll not have slept much while he was captive. That would be Blaze." Brody walked towards the couch, a hand resting on his son's head as he prayed, thanking God for bringing Blaze home but also for protection for the young couple. They were far from done with their adventure, he surmised, and his thoughts would be correct.

None of the occupants of the house heard the subtle noises outside as men moved in and then moved away. The men's frustration was evident. They needed to take Blaze back with them and also to bring Bevin with them. That wasn't happening at the moment. They stared at Frank's patrol vehicle, hatred on their faces that the police were already there in the cabin. That was not to have happened.

Chapter 35

Frank walked towards Blaze as that man roused, a cup of coffee extended towards him. Blaze sat up, frowning at Frank even as he rubbed at his face. He was on his feet, heading for the bathroom, needing to wash and prepare for the day. Frank watched him walk away before his head dropped. Blaze was avoiding him for the moment but that could not last. He really needed to hear what Blaze had to say before he spoke with Bevin or any of the parents.

Blaze stared at himself in the mirror over the sink, seeing the ravages of what he had been through. He was not the same man that he had been, he had to acknowledge. He had fought out his captivity with his Heavenly Father and knew that God had released him and brought him home. He just had to deal with what he had been through.

Turning at last to walk back to the living room, he found Frank staring out of the living room window, no sign of any impatience around him. That was Frank, Blaze knew, patient to the point of not moving.

"Frank?" Blaze watched as Frank turned to him. "You need to speak with me."

"I do, Blaze. We need to speak before you say anything to your parents, Brenna, or Bevin." Frank frowned as Bevin appeared and reached for Blaze. He smiled to himself. She was not leaving him, not even when Blaze gave his statement. For now, he would allow that. They were newlyweds who had been torn apart by cruel, evil men. "How be we sit for now?

Bevin, you can stay but if I need you to leave at any point, then you must."

Bevin nodded. She just didn't want to have to leave Blaze's side. She wanted to know what had transpired to keep him away from her and that could only happen at the present time by staying quiet.

Blaze sat, his arm pulling Bevin as tight to him as he could. He sighed. He had no idea where to start or what to say. He reached for the cup of coffee sitting on the table beside him and sipped, trying to gather his thoughts. He just didn't know if he could and if he did, if they would make any sense. Somehow, Blaze had to tell his story and he wasn't sure what to say to make it clear what had happened. That was totally unlike him. He was normally a clear and concise thinker and speaker. This had changed that for him and he didn't like it, not one bit.

Frank nodded. He had worked with other victims of crime almost too much, he decided. Blaze was troubled by what he needed to say. Frank would let him take the time he needed to compose his thoughts and then speak.

"Blaze? Just start speaking. I'll video tape your statement as well as record it and also take my notes. Just talk. I'll clarify anything that I need to when you're finished. I will also be back speaking with you time and time again." Frank gave a grim smile as Blaze shook his head.

"That's what I'm afraid of, Frank, that you won't leave me alone about it. I don't know if I can tell what happened more than once." Blaze's eyes closed as he tried to sort out the muddle of his thoughts. It just didn't seem possible. "Okay, to go back to that day. I was taken from here. Three men just appeared and forced me into a truck. There was a driver keeping the truck waiting for us. One man sat on each side of me. They were gruff speaking and scruffily dressed, similar to what you would see with hard labourers. I wasn't able to move, a weapon poking into my side. Before we left, a blindfold was dropped over my eyes. I couldn't tell you what direction we went. They seemed to be driving in circles, more than likely to confuse me."

Blaze thought back over those first few moments being blindfolded and a captive. He had felt fear rising in his heart and prayed for release. When release didn't come, he prayed for peace and protection. Blaze was terrified for Bevin, afraid that they would come after her and take her away from him and that he would never see her again.

Feeling the truck slowing and then making a turn onto a rough surface, Blaze grew more afraid. It was not his character to be afraid but this was different. He was threatened with death and could feel the weapon digging into his side. He didn't dare move, hearing the mutters from the men but not understanding their words. Blaze waited for whatever was to come, praying for safety and protection.

A hand on his upper arm drew him roughly from the truck and to his feet. He stumbled as he landed on the ground, unable to sense what was around him or to see what he was landing on. The same hand propelled him rapidly forward, despite his protest that he needed to see where he was going. Those protests were ignored.

Blaze could sense that he was now inside a building but not what kind of building or what it was like inside. Instead, he was shoved down onto a chair, the blindfold still in place. His wrists were bound to the chair arms, leaving him feeling very vulnerable, something that he didn't know if he had ever felt before.

Time passed as Blaze waited for whatever it was to happen. He could hear footsteps around him, echoing slightly on the hard wooden floor. He could also hear the mutters once more of the men but none of them came near him. There was some light coming in around the end of the blindfold but it was across his eyes in such a way that he could not glimpse anything.

Blaze was finally released from the chair and hauled to his feet, once more roughly. He was then shoved forward, stumbling again as he tried to keep his balance. A hard shove on his back sent him flying forward to land heavily and awkwardly on the wooden floor of a room, his head hitting hard and sending him spiralling downwards into darkness.

The man who had shoved him stared at Blaze before he sneered and slammed and locked the door behind him. Blaze was where he was to be, for now. Their employer had left specific instructions on how long to keep him bound to the chair and then what to do with him after that length of time. His thinking was that this would wear Blaze down quickly and he would be compliant with his demands. This evil man didn't take into consideration that God was with Blaze and was protecting him even then. He just didn't consider God to be worth thinking about.

Blaze roused late that night, not moving for a moment before he raised himself to a sitting position. He listened carefully for sounds of anyone around him and heard nothing. A shaky hand reached for the blindfold and removed it. Blaze blinked as his eyes adjusted to the dimness of the room lit only by a single low light bulb hanging from a simple ceiling fixture. Blaze was on his feet in short order, searching for a way out. He tugged at the door, not able to open it. Approaching the windows, Blaze stopped. He could not go near them. God was preventing that, he knew. His instincts told him that someone was out there, waiting for him to try and escape. And if he tried that, Blaze was certain that he would be harmed.

Blaze sighed. He had no idea where he was or why he had been taken. He could only pray for comfort, protection and release for himself and for protection for his beloved Bevin. His prayer was that she was safe and unharmed.

Chapter 36

The next morning, Blaze was awakened by a rough shove at his shoulder. He had not planned to sleep but he had. God had provided peace for him in his captivity and he had sought out the rough pallet of blankets on the floor. His prayer as he had drifted off had been for release and then for Bevin.

Rousing, Blaze rubbed at his face before he was roughly hauled to his feet and shoved from the room. He stumbled somewhat as he regained his footing, not sure why this was happening or who had been behind it all.

Forced to stand in an empty room, Blaze just prayed. That was all that he could do. He didn't hear anyone around him but was wise enough not to move. The threats that had come at him ensured that he didn't. He had not idea how long he had been there before the same rough hands shoved him back into the room.

Blaze stood for a moment, swaying on his feet before he sought out the pallet and collapsed. He checked his watch. It had been hours that he had been kept standing there. Blaze was well aware of what the men were trying to do. He had heard stories like this all too often.

He didn't raise his head as the door opened and a tray was set not the floor. He was deep in prayer by this time, waiting for his Heavenly Father to touch him and bring more peace and comfort to him.

The man who stood in the doorway was puzzled. Blaze was not reacting as they all expected him to. He wasn't trying to escape or fight with them. Instead, he just waited. And what he was waiting for, none of them was sure about. Their employer had been around when Blaze had been in the empty room, watching him with hatred and violence evident on his face. He fully expected Blaze to fight back but he too was puzzled when Blaze didn't.

This went on every few hours with Blaze pulled from the locked room and forced to stand in the empty room. He was growing fatigued, not allowed to rest even when he was locked away. The light was never shut off. There was low music that played all the time, heavy on the drum sounds. He was given barely enough food for a meal.

Blaze was growing weak and weary. He claimed the verse that spoke about being like an eagle and not growing weary even though he was. Blaze could feel a presence with him no matter which room he was in and knew that God had sent an angel to protect and guide him in his responses. He was never asked for anything or asked to do anything. Blaze knew what the men were up to. He just wasn't going to help them out. He refused to speak even when blows would hit his body.

Finally on his feet in the locked room, as unsteady as he was, Blaze searched once more for a way to escape. He had the strongest impression that he needed to get away right then or he would not survive. He had heard the faint murmurings that he wasn't supposed to hear. If he didn't cooperate with the men,

Blaze's life would be forfeited. And that he was do his best to avoid.

He reached for the door knob, not expecting the door to open. He hesitated for a moment before he stepped outside, listening for anyone who might be in the house. Blaze could hear no sounds of any human around him. He crept towards an outside door, opening it and then stepping outside. The sun blinded him for a moment before Blaze looked around and then just headed for the back of the property and to safety and freedom.

Blaze turned as he reached the back of the yard, staring at the house behind him. He sighed. He knew who it belonged to. That man had been rumoured for years to be on the take from criminals. No one person had been able to prove it. It figures, he thought, that it was up to him to do that. Blaze would be reaching back out to friends for their help. But first, he needed to find someone to get him back to his cabin and to his beloved bride.

Blaze came back to the present and faced Frank. He could not explain how he managed to reach his cabin. Someone had helped him. Only he had no idea who that person was. They had found him staggering along the road and stopped. Blaze didn't remember the drive back to the cabin, only that the person had brought him home and then helped him inside before leaving. Blaze made a decision at that point that he would not look too hard for the man. God had provided a way home for him and that was that.

"I don't know who it was, Frank." Blaze kept his eyes steady on Frank who was frowning at him. "I really don't. I was so tired by that time that I don't even remember the drive back here. You have my statement. I can't add anything to it. I never saw the men's faces. They made sure of that. I can tell you where I was and you'll know who was behind it. We just have to prove it."

Frank nodded, writing down the address. He drew in a deep breath. From what he knew, Blaze was fortunate to still be alive. That man was deep into criminal activities. They had just never been able to prove it despite arrests made of those connected to him. Those arrested refused to talk.

Walking away at last, Frank frowned once more. He paused his forward walk, turning to stare back at the cabin. It was late evening and the low lights in the cabin shone faintly around the drapes. Frank raised his face to the sky, feeling the soft cool breeze that wafted across it. He stared at the moon and the stars, thanking God for providing release from Blaze. He just had no idea where he went from there. The sounds of nature filled his ears as he turned back to his car, heading away from the cabin and towards home. Frank was exhausted but not as much as Blaze was. He just had no answers for either Blaze or Bevin.

Blaze turned from locking the door, finding Bevin standing right behind him. She walked into his hug, holding on and just grateful to whoever it was who had helped Blaze.

"Blaze? What do we do now?" Bevin was at a loss as to where they went in their own investigation.

"We meet with our friends, Ashlynn and the girls. Other friends will want to move in as well. Torin reached out and asked that we meet at his home in two days. That will let me get back up to where I need to be at work." Blaze stared down at the face turned up to his before he kissed his lady. "And I want you there to work with me on it. We need to do this, sweetheart."

"I know that we do. This is where it gets more dangerous for us, Blaze, my love. They will come looking for you since you escaped from their jail cell that they prepared for you."

Blaze frowned down at Bevin, taken aback somewhat by her words. His eyes raised as he studied the cabin, not sure that they should still be there but knowing that they needed that time alone.

———

Chapter 37

Two days later, Bevin turned from the door to look around the main cabin. They had moved back there the night before, not because they wanted to but because they felt that they had to. Mary and Art had moved to the little cabin a ways from the main cabin, something that they had always planned on doing. Blaze had just hugged Mary as she stated that, knowing that she was correct in her words.

Bevin watched as so many people seemed to have invaded their home. Ashlynn was watching her and moved in to hug her.

"There are a lot of people in your home, Bevin, but they are here to support both you and Blaze. We want this over for you and over in the next day or so." She grinned as Bevin snorted. "You don't think that can happen?"

"I know it can, if it's in God's will for us. And I pray that it is. This took too much from Blaze. He's hurting because he thinks that it's someone he trusted."

"And it likely is. Blaze doesn't trust easily, given what he does and unfortunately, because of his wealth." Ashlynn's hand went up to still Bevin's words. "Torin is the same way. Neither man trusts easily. And it is how it should be." She turned Bevin towards the living room. "Go and find your fellow. The girls are looking after our coffees, teas, and food. It's what they do."

"I know. I had a long talk with Brinn the other night. She called just to talk. You raised some beautiful and very thoughtful ladies, Ashlynn." Bevin walked away to where Blaze stood waiting for her, to wrap her into a hug before he tugged her down onto a seat. He dropped at her feet, his arm resting on her knee.

"Torin? Can we spend some time in prayer? We need that." Blaze's quiet voice seemed to echo through the room as everyone found seats and then grew quiet.

"We can do that. And you do need that, Blaze and Bevin, and your families as well." Torin paused as he studied Brenna. William had not reappeared nor had anyone heard from him. That was concerning to them all as they had no idea if he was working against them or was held against his will. Bevin had shaken her head and walked away when Torin had questioned her.

Brody was on his feet at one point, searching for Bevin. He found her just standing on the back deck, an arm around one of the upright posts. He paused beside her, seeing how lost in thought that she was.

Bevin turned at last. She had been aware that Brody stood beside her and had waited for him to speak. She sighed to herself when he didn't and finally turned to him. She found him staring as well at the back of the yard, not ready to speak.

"Brody? You have a question?" Bevin's voice was low. Brody could heard the stress and fear in it.

"I do. I'm just now sure how to ask it." Brody prayed for his daughter-in-law. He was so afraid that something would happen to her and she would either disappear or be killed. He knew how hard that would be on his son if that happened.

"Just ask it. I may be able to answer it or I may not. I can't tell unless you speak." Bevin gave him a quick grin, finding himself smiling in return.

"Okay. You're not from this town. You were brought here for a reason. That reason seems to be Blaze. Did you know of Blaze or his charities before that?" Brody waited patiently for Bevin to speak, listening to the afternoon sounds of nature that usually calmed him. Today, they weren't and that troubled him.

"Did I know of Blaze before this?" Bevin studied the man whom she now considered a father figure in her life. She shook her head. "I don't know that I did. His name? No, I had never heard of it before. And his charities? Not one." Bevin was troubled by why she had been brought there. "There was nothing to connect the two of us at all. That's what is so puzzling and troubling about all this. How were we connected? Do you know?" Bevin was praying that he did.

Brody shook his head. He had no idea how the couple had been connected but connected in one way they had been.

"It's just puzzling why you were brought to his office building. If you didn't know him, there would have been no reason for that to happen."

"That's what I don't get." Bevin began to pace, Brody turning slightly to watch her, a concerned look on his face. "How did I end up there? I didn't intentionally go there. I was taken to close to there and then released. I ran that way, seeing the building and praying that I could find someone to help. The men caught up with me before that happened. You know what happened next."

"We do." Frank had come to find the pair. "And it's troubling to say the least that you were brought here, against your will, to a town and building that could have meant grave harm to you." Frank pointed back into the cabin. "In you go, Bevin. We have word that someone is heading this way that means both of you harm." He watched as she stared at him in horror before she ran to find Blaze.

Brody watched her leave before he spoke to Frank.

"Frank? What do we do? How do we keep them safe?"

"We can't keep them totally safe. I can't put an officer with them all the time. Friends with security teams are weighing and will be moving in to provide security as of tomorrow. Blaze and Bevin won't see them but they will be there. It's when they're on their own that it will be difficult. And we can't have someone with them all day, every day."

"No, we can't. Neither one of them will accept that." Brody walked away, lost in thought, trying to come up with a name or company that he could provide to Frank that would end all of this for his son and his bride and not able to do that.

Frank sighed. He was no further ahead with his investigation despite any and all information that had been provided to him. He needed that one piece that he didn't have and needed. He walked away from the cabin, heading for his car. The vibration of his phone stopped him in his tracks as he pulled it. The email that he had received from Emma was what he needed, he decided, on the run for his car and then headed for his office.

Blaze watched as Frank's car disappeared. He had a question himself for Frank that would now have to wait. His phone was out as he sent off a text message to Frank, asking if he had investigated his security team. Blaze had a suspicion that one of them was on the take as it was said and it wanted it proven or disproven.

Chapter 38

Early the next morning, Frank was headed back towards Blaze and Bevin. Word had been confirmed that someone would attempt to harm the couple that morning, and Frank was determined not to let it happen, if he could possibly manage that. He pulled to a stop near the end of the driveway, searching through the dimness. A sudden exclamation was torn from him and he was running towards a dark form that lay on the ground outside of the cabin.

Frank was on his knees, his hands reaching to turn the body over. Horror shot through him for a moment as he realized that it was Blaze. A quick call for help sounded over his police radio before he was assessing Blaze. Blaze was alive but unconscious. On his feet, Frank ran for the cabin and searched it swiftly. It was as he had feared. Bevin had disappeared.

Back outside, Frank watched as the paramedics worked on Blaze before he was loaded into an ambulance and disappeared. George stood beside him, shock on his face for a moment.

"Where's Bevin?"

"She's not here. I have no idea where she is." Frank was frustrated. This is what he had tried to avoid but had been unable to do that. "We need to search for her." The chiming of his phone had him muttering before he pulled it out. A hand stopped George from moving away. "Will and Bob have come through. They are watching a van right now that has Bevin in it." Frank was away, George watching as he drove off.

―――

George's duty was at the cabin. Frank's duty was to find the van and then work to release Bevin before she was seriously injured or killed.

Frank's thoughts turned to prayers for his friends. This was not how the day was to be, he knew, but God was there and in control. He had to trust Him to lead.

Finding Will and Bob, Frank paused beside them, his eyes on the van that had been parked outside of a fence that surrounded a wealthy home. Frank knew who the owner of the home was and sighed. This just complicated it even more. That man was part of the board of one of Blaze's charities and knew full well how to get to Blaze without too much difficulty.

"Have they moved Bevin?" Frank kept his voice low, not knowing if any of the man's employees were around them.

"No. They have just parked it here and left it. Bob snuck up and peeked inside. Bevin is in there, tied up, but on her own. How do you want to do this, Frank?"

Frank nodded. It would be his call to free her and that needed to be done quickly.

"Are the doors locked?" The van was an older model without key fobs to open it.

"They are but a friend from the street has already unlocked it." Bob looked around before he was running for the van, sliding open the door and reaching to gather Bevin into his arms. He was back across the street, heading for Frank's car with Will and Frank chasing after him.

Frank drove off, Will and Bob flanking Bevin in the back seat even as those two men worked to free her. He caught a glimpse of the anger that Bevin was feeling and smiled to himself. She had every right to be angry.

"Frank? Blaze? Is he okay?" Bevin's worry for her groom came through in her voice.

"I don't know, Bevin. I found him and then found you missing. He's at the hospital. We'll head there and you will be assessed as well. That is not an option." Frank parked near the ambulance bays and was out of the car and walking Bevin inside. Will and Bob nodded at him before they disappeared, off to watch that house again. Frank nodded in response, knowing that they would reach out to him as they could.

Bevin impatiently sat through her assessment and then turned to Frank. Frank simply pointed to an empty room and with a hand on her arm, directed her there.

"I need your statement before you speak with anyone else, including Blaze." Frank stood in front of the closed door, watching Bevin as she paced. She was angry but also afraid, he knew. He had seen it too many times.

"Talk to me, Bevin. What happened?"

"What happened?" Bevin spun to glare at Frank. It wasn't his fault, she knew, but she had to release her feelings. "We were out on the front porch, enjoying the early morning and our coffee when that van drove up. We didn't have a chance. I was grabbed and almost thrown into the van. Blaze tried to stop them but he went down. I don't know how or why. They bound and gagged me before they drove off. I can't give a description of the three men. They were wearing disguises, just like they always do. Now, can I see Blaze?" She stomped towards him, stopping as he held up his hand.

"In a moment. Just to clarify, you didn't see the men enough to identify them?"

"No. I can't." Bevin simply reached around Frank and pulled open the door, searching for Blaze. Finding him, she almost ran to his bedside, a hand out to rest on his as her other hand rested on his hair.

Blaze turned slightly, sensing Bevin was near. His eyes flickered open as he searched for the men who had taken him down. The surprise of their appearing had prevented him from protecting his bride. He had chased after them, one of the men turning and simply tackling him, a hard blow to his head rendering him unconscious. He was surprised to find himself in the hospital.

"Blaze?" Bevin kept her voice low, just in case someone heard her.

"Bevin?" Blaze turned towards her, a hand rising to touch her cheek. "You're free?"

"I am. Frank, Will, and Bob found me. But you? How are you? And when can you go home?" Bevin turned as she heard footsteps and Brody and Emily appeared. "He's okay and so am I."

Brody and Emily simply hugged the couple as they waited from them to move. Frank had found them, asking that they keep the couple safe but knowing that it was likely impossible to do.

"Where are you heading, Blaze?" Brody asked the question that was hovering in the room.

"I don't know, Dad. They seem to be able to find us no matter where we are. And we need to stay safe for the next few days." Blaze's head went back. "We'll pack some stuff and move to the apartment in the building. At least there, we should be safe."

"But there are no guarantees of that, is there?" Brody was well aware that there had been a breach in their security but no one had been able to pinpoint just who it was that had done that.

"I know, Dad. I know. We'll do what we can. But what about you and Mom?"

"They're not after us, son. You are the one that they are after. And I for one would like to know why." Emily had thoughts on who it was and stated the names of those whom she suspected.

Both Bevin and Blaze stared at her before they were nodding. They would need to meet and plan how to bring those people down. And that meant reaching out further to other friends who had already been in touch with them.

———

Chapter 39

A day later, Frank walked towards Blaze and Bevin where they stood outside of the office building. They had chosen not to hide, knowing that if they did, it would only delay the inevitable. And they wanted it over. They wanted to be able to move freely with their life and that wasn't possible.

Frank studied them, sensing something different about them that day. He sighed. He was exhausted. There were just too many cases for the investigators and their case loads just kept growing.

"Frank? Have you arrested the head person yet?" Blaze went right to the core of what they needed to now.

"No, we haven't. We're still gathering information on that person. How did you ever come up with the name?" Frank was puzzled at that,

"I don't know, Frank. God, I guess." Blaze pointed behind him. "And we are being watched even now. As you arrest someone, someone else moves in. How many people does he have working for him?"

"Far too many, I think, Blaze. Now, you're out here in the open. What are your plans?" Frank gave a brief grin as Blaze and Bevin shared a look.

"We're not sitting around here, that's for sure, Frank." Blaze reached for Bevin's hand. "We're putting ourselves out there. We want this over and over now." Blaze tamped down his anger, knowing that he had to take that to God. He could feel God's presence with them and knew that He was protecting them. Blaze tugged on Bevin's hand to move her forward without taking his eyes from Frank. He frowned when she just didn't respond. "Bevin?"

"Blaze? Frank? I don't think that we are going anywhere, at least not of our own free will." Bevin watched as the half dozen men moved in around them. "I would say that we are in a standoff." She nodded behind Frank, drawing Blaze's and Frank's attention to the men.

"This is not what we wanted, Blaze, Bevin." Frank was angry and frustrated. At the moment, he was unable to respond to the danger, only able to watch and gauge who would be the most dangerous man there. He could also only pray for safety and protection for his friends and himself.

No one was willing to make the first move. Blaze stood, his hand tight on Bevin's, as they watched first Frank and then the men around them. His eyes lifted as he saw others moving in, breathing a sigh of relief that those approaching were officers. He just had to keep his head and keep his lady safe. That wasn't something that Blaze was confident that he could do.

Bevin watched the men, sensing that help was on the way or nearby. She frowned as she recognized some of the men and sighed. Of course they would be friends of her father's. And just how did that relate to him? Was he behind this all?

"I know the men." Bevin kept her voice low enough that only Frank and Blaze heard her. "They're friends of my father."

"They are? That explains what we were finding then." Frank's hand rested on his weapon. He knew that the head of it all was among the men. He recognized each one of them. "Walter Jones. You are under arrest."

Walter Jones gave a hoarse laugh. He knew that Frank was on his own, or so he surmised. He didn't see or hear the men with him being placed under arrest and then led away. He was arrogant enough to assume that no one would touch him. Jones jumped as he felt hands on his wrists, drawing them behind him, and then clapping steel handcuffs on him.

"What is the meaning of this? I am only here to discuss business with a friend." Jones spluttered as he was turned away from the trio in front of him, shoved across the parking lot, and then into a patrol vehicle.

Frank didn't relax until all the men were taken away. He turned slightly to face the couple, seeing the questions on their faces.

"This is it, Blaze, Bevin. We have all of them now. Give us a couple of days to sort through everything and then we'll meet. God was here, protecting you. I felt His angels around us just now." Frank walked away, a hand out for the papers that were being offered to him.

Blaze wrapped Bevin into his arms, his chin resting on her head. Both of them were in shock, not fully comprehending that it was all over. They were certain that someone else was out there.

"Is this it?" Bevin finally breathed life to the thoughts that they were struggling with.

"Frank seems to think so. I guess it is." Blaze was still in shock about what had just transpired. "Did that really happen?"

"It did." Bevin looked around at the security personnel who now surrounded them. "Can we go home, Blaze, or do you need to be in the office?"

"I need to be in the office for a couple of hours. Then, we'll head for home and lock ourselves in." Blaze kissed his lady before turning her back to the building. "We'll be safe here for now. Thank you, Bevin, for being who you are."

Late that night, Blaze looked up from where he had taken a seat on the back deck, reaching out a hand for his lady. She snuggled close to him, not saying a word, simply listening to the night sounds.

"Frank called when you were in the shower." Blaze broke the silence at last. "He found your father."

"He did? And what excuse did Dad have?" Bevin waited for Blaze to speak, finally turning to find a sober, sad look on his face. "Blaze?"

"Your dad is really sick, sweetheart. He has hidden that fact for years from you and your mother. That is part of why he was like he was with you two. He was afraid to tell you that his condition is terminal. He doesn't have long left to live." Blaze tightened his arms around his bride, feeling the sobs as they started. "We'll meet up with him in the next day or so. Your mom is with him right now."

"And he never said anything. He should have. We should have known." Bevin's emotions finally slowed down as she slept, content in the arms of her groom.

Chapter 40

A week later, Frank walked towards the main cabin, studying the vehicles that were parked there. For once, he didn't have a sense of danger that had surrounded Blaze and Bevin. Their adventure, as it was called, was over without them facing the life and death situations that so many others had faced. God had been gracious in that way, protecting them from that.

Blaze reached to shake Frank's hand, knowing that the detective would share what he could. Other information and facts would stay hidden until the trials were over and those facts could come out.

"Thank you, Frank. You have been a blessing and Godsend through all of this." Blaze turned to face the cabin. "Bevin is around somewhere."

Frank laughed. He had received a text message from that lady, just asking if he was coming for the meal and what could she prepare as a thank you for him.

"She was in touch. She wanted to know what she could prepare for me as a meal." Frank had come to appreciate the sense of humour and caring and compassion that made up that lady. Sue was becoming a good friend of hers, much to Bevin's delight.

"She would do that. It's who she is. We're looking at setting up a company or charity for her to use those very attributes. It's still in the planning stages." Blaze shut the door behind him, hearing the laughter and happiness that sounded through the cabin. "We're meeting in the living room or outside, whichever suits best."

"The living room works. It's starting to cloud over and the wind is picking up." Bevin appeared to hug Frank before she was away again, not content to sit still or stay in one spot.

"You need to corner your bride, Blaze." Frank laughed at him as he moved away to greet the friends and family that had gathered with them. The only sadness that seemed to hang over the group was that Bevin's father was in palliative care and could not be there. Frank knew that Bevin was hurting in many ways because of that man and he had directed her to someone to speak with. She had been grateful for that.

An hour later, their meal over, Blaze stood and looked around, waiting for everyone to quiet down.

"Frank is here to give as much as he can on the investigation. Before that, we need to spend time in prayer. Dad? Will you start us off?" Blaze hugged his father before he was seated beside his bride, his head bowing as his father began to pray.

Frank looked around at last, not sure how to start or even where to start.

"I'm not sure where or how to start. Brody, this goes back a ways, back to your father in fact. Your dad? He made the millions, did he not?"

Brody nodded. He could still remember the years of not having enough until his father's investments began to pay off. He also remembered the conversations that he had had with his parents, that the money that they were making was God's and that they had to use it for Him. He had been in complete agreement with that. When the millions had passed on to him, that was exactly how he continued to run the company, expanding to charity work as Blaze joined him.

"That's correct. He also was adamant that the money was God's. He would not use it for anything else but that. He lived frugally as do we."

Frank was nodding. He was well aware of that. He had spoken with those around the family and that was what he had been told.

"But I don't see how Walter Jones comes into this." Blaze was puzzled. He had not known the man and had approached his father about him. Brody had shaken his head. He didn't know the man either.

"He's your age, Brody. You didn't know him but he grew up in your town, watching as you seemed to have an easy and wealthy lifestyle. He was from what we would call the other side of the tracks, from a family that did nothing but fight, with a father who cheated repeatedly on his wife, and was physically and emotionally abusive to his family. Jones followed you one day just for curiosity and saw your home and how your parents treated you. He was jealous. That jealousy continued to fester inside him. He turned to crime to try and gain wealth but it never worked out as he thought it would. The money left him dissatisfied with life. The jealousy led him into avenues that your charities fought against. I won't and can't go into them at this time but they will come out in his trial. He

---

blamed you, Brody, and decided that to ruin Blaze would ruin you. Except we know how that worked out." Frank grew silent. He could say no more.

No one was able to explain how William's friends had connected with Jones. They weren't talking and Jones wasn't either, unable to because of his mental state. There was also no explanation as to why Bevin had been chased from town to town until she ended up at Blaze's office.

Frank rose at last, leaving conversation behind him. He walked from the cabin, turning as he heard Bevin calling his name.

Bevin simply hugged Frank and thanked him, a prayer whispered for him. She watched as he drove away, feeling Blaze's arms around her.

"He's tired, Blaze."

"He is but he won't stop, sweetheart. He needs to keep going. Solving crime is who he is. One day, he'll retire but now is not the time." He kissed her cheek. "Have I told you today that I love you?"

A year later, Blaze was on a hunt for Bevin. He had searched the office building, not finding her there. The security guard on duty had laughed and stated that she had left an hour before. Could Blaze not keep track of his wife? Blaze had laughed in return, stating that he normally could. The relationship between Blaze and his security team was such that they could tease one another without any hard feelings.

Stepping into the cabin, Blaze could hear Bevin singing softly to herself. He dropped his briefcase in his office and then headed to change out of his suit. He had had meetings today and needed to be dressed formally.

Hunting for Bevin, he found her curled up on the glider on the back deck. He just sat beside her and drew her into his arms, kissing her as he did so. He fell more and more in love with his lady each day.

"Have a good day, sweetheart?" Blaze waited for Bevin to speak.

"I did. I met with some of the ladies who had stories to tell. We're working on a book and then some teaching material. We want to train others to be there for those who go through trouble, to be the hands and feet of God on earth for them." Bevin had helped to create just such a charity and was seeing it growing week by week. She felt blessed that God was using her in such a way, a way that she had not expected.

"That's wonderful. God is certainly blessing that work." Blaze grew quiet, content just to sit and listen to the sounds of nature around them. "There's something else."

"There is. Mom was around just before you came. She's heading back home. She feels that's where God wants her. I'll miss her but I understand." Bevin's head rested against her groom. "When we have children, she says that she'll move back here."

"That she will. And God's timing on that is His timing." Blaze and Bevin were praying for a family but were waiting on God's timing. "I am so thankful that He protected us as He did."

"Me, too. Without Him, we would not have survived. That was what Jones wanted. He wanted to kill you and then me just to get back at your dad. And I still don't fully understand his reasoning."

"None of us do. Unfortunately, we'll never fully understand why. With his mental status the way it is, he'll never go to trial. And that leaves a lot of unanswered questions."

"It does. But God had a plan and purpose for what we went through. And He is still working out that plan and purpose."

The couple grew quiet, knowing that Bevin's words were true. There was still a part of them that wanted to know the real reasons for what they had been put through. They had to leave that with their God.

"I love you, Mrs. Framer. Will you go out for dinner with me?" Blaze reached to kiss his sweetheart.

"I love you too, Mr. Framer. And yes, I will." Bevin made no move to rise, knowing that if they didn't get out for a meal in a restaurant that night, it would happen at some point. Neither one was worried about that. And that God was blessing their work through the charities that they had. That was their daily prayer, that they reached others for Him.

Thank you for choosing to read the story of Blaze and his beloved bride, Bevin. Blaze was a secondary character in Brinn's story, friends with her sister, Darbi. There was never any attention to write his story. Unruly characters have a way of having that happened, and Blaze was no different.

Blaze and Bevin truly did need God's protection as they struggled to understand why and who. As always, it is at the end of their story that the culprit and reason become clear. The theme of the story is how God protects and provides for them even in time of danger. With Blaze, his millions made no difference in how he reacted to danger or how he tried hard to protect his lady.

As always, characters from other stories just have to become part of another's adventures. As one of the ladies stated, they like to tag along on anyone else's adventures. This time? It was Abe and Emma from *His Guardians*, Blackie and Julia and Simon and Eavan from *Mistletoe Treasures*, Ashlynn and her four girls from *His Ladies with the Lamps*, Richard from *His Protectors*, and Don from *His Defenders*. These characters always add to the story and help to move the story line along.

God truly does protect us and does indeed have a plan and purpose for our lives. We will never likely know here on earth what we were protected from or how He used us to forward His plans for His people. All we can do is place our hand in His and follow His leading. We need to be the hands and feet for Him on earth.

God bless each one of you as you walk forward in your life for Him.

217

Ronna

9 781998 821532